Praise for

NO MAN'S LAND

"Grave, gentle, devastating ..."
The Globe and Mail

"An exceptional novel that you will read and
treasure and tell your friends about."
The Evening Telegram

"... a brilliant treatment ... the writing is
exceptional ... *No Man's Land* treats one of
Newfoundland's and Canada's bitterest
experiences with dignity and truthfulness."
Halifax Chronicle-Herald

"A masterful account of the Battle of the
Somme ... a pleasure to hold and read."
Journal of Adolescent & Adult Literacy

"As a literary evocation of the Great War, *No
Man's Land* belongs on the same shelf as
David Macfarlane's *The Danger Tree* and
Timothy Findley's *The Wars*."
Toronto Star

NO MAN'S LAND

Kevin Major

Anchor Canada

National Library of Canada Cataloguing in Publication Data

Major, Kevin, 1949-
    No man's land

ISBN 0-385-65886-9

1. Somme, 1st Battle of the, France, 1916—Fiction.
2. World War, 1914-1918—Fiction. I. Title.

PS8576.A523N6 2001   C813'.54   C2001-900756-6
PR9199.3.M34554N6 2001

Cover photograph courtesy The Provincial Archives of
    Newfoundland and Labrador
Hand tinting of cover photo by Manfred Buchheit Photography
Cover design by David Montle
Text design by Heidy Lawrance Associates
Printed and bound in Canada

Published in Canada by
Anchor Canada, a division of
Random House of Canada Limited

Visit Random House of Canada Limited's website:
www.randomhouse.ca

TRANS 10 9 8 7

In memory of the young men of the Newfoundland Regiment who went off to the Great War, and for the families they left.

For the family of my youth—Ina, Roland, Mona, Maxine, Carl, and Minette; Louise, Murray, Mark, Norma, and Gerald; and for their children and grandchildren.

Hayward went to bed, Gallipoli in his mind.

The fellow who had relieved him on sentry duty was too young for the regiment. He had lied to be one of the First Five Hundred. A devil-may-care, brazen sort, Hayward remembered, heedless enough to light a cigarette.

"No sign of Johnny Turk," Hayward had said. Still, he could never have expected the fellow to sneak a look over the parapet.

The sniper's bullet took him in the forehead, above an eye, tearing open his skull just below the rim of his tin hat. He toppled from the fire-step, flat on his back, the cigarette still burning between his lips.

Hayward did nothing at first, his back pressed against the trench wall.

He reached to the fellow's mouth and extracted the cigarette. He fell back, away from him, and did not look his way again. He called for stretcher-bearers and, clutching his rifle, resumed sentry duty until there were orders for a replacement.

ONE

Sunlight through cracks in the shutters woke him. He was surprised to have slept through the night. On his side, his hands wedged between his knees, his leaden greatcoat over him, Hayward listened for explosions on the German front lines. He lifted his head rigidly off the pillow, but could hear only faint fire. It left him doubtful that the artillery had been as relentless as on the nights before.

Outside the window a horse and cart sloshed through the farmyard mud and onto the road. On the other side of the room, Clarke stirred in his bed. The officer turned over, cursed, mumbled something about cutting wire and fell back to sleep.

Hayward remembered how at home he would lie under piles of bedclothes, warm and secretive. And how his mother laid out home-made bread and rhubarb jam for him when he came down the stairs to breakfast.

She would sit across the table while he ate it, drinking tea and talking with him about what the lady customers had bought at the Water Street store where he worked.

He felt along the floor until his hand came upon his folded breeches. From a pocket he retrieved his watch. His father had given it to him the day he boarded the *Florizel* and sailed for the war. The face had several deep scratches, but it had survived the trenches in Gallipoli when others had not, and it still kept good time. It showed seven minutes past five.

Silently he brought his feet to the floor and sat up. His greatcoat fell away stiffly. With his shoulders hunched, he crossed his hands in front of his chest and rubbed them along his upper arms. A shiver ran through him. He quickly pulled on the new woollen socks he had been saving. Over the past couple of weeks officers in other regiments would have paid him well for such fine home-knit socks, but their offers had not been any temptation.

He put his legs into his breeches, stood up and fastened them around his waist, taking care that his undervest was well tucked inside, then slipped the braces over his shoulders. His shaving kit, towel, and Sam Browne belt in his hand, he left the room with Clarke still asleep.

Near the head of the stairs was the washstand, and on it a porcelain basin, filled with water to where its lip was broken away. On the floor stood a water bucket, a wooden ladle floating inside. Normally the water would have been much colder. He was pleased to think that Madame had kept the bucket by the fire downstairs to let the chill out of it.

He went to a window and pushed open the shutters part way for more light, careful that anybody who might be outside would not see him in his undervest. There was a bright, cloudless sky. How relieved the whole regiment would be now that the rain had finally stopped.

When he finished washing, a grey scum floated in the basin.

His Sam Browne served as a strop to sharpen the razor. He made a thin lather with his shaving brush and soap and bent his head closer to the broken piece of mirror that hung on the wall.

Before making the first stroke, he stared at his hand holding the blade. With concentration he steadied it. Even so, by the time he had finished there were two rivulets of blood on his face. He wiped them off with the towel and rubbed his shaving stick against the nicks. He took no notice of the burning.

The contents of the basin he poured out the window. He gathered his kit and went quietly back into the room to finish dressing.

Just before starting down the stairs, he positioned himself in front of the fragment of mirror. He always liked his appearance in uniform, since the days as a schoolboy in St. John's when he joined the Methodist Guards. His mother always smiled and said how smart and proper he looked, his father nodding his agreement.

Now he wore a brass-buttoned tunic over a khaki shirt and tie. His breeches ended just below the knee, and from there to his ankle boots were strapped leather gaiters, covering his puttees. A strap across his chest held a leather case, and inside, his pistol. His cap, and the collar of his tunic, bore the caribou badge of the Newfoundland Regiment, and the one embroidered star inside the braiding on the cuffs of his tunic confirmed the rank of second lieutenant. The past few months had dulled the uniform, despite his best efforts during his days away from the trenches, and he expected it would be some time before a new one would be issued. For a few seconds he stood with his ash-stick, before putting it away and starting down the stairs.

It was a warm kitchen he entered. Madame Cornot looked up, continuing to stir the steaming pot on the wood stove.

She had the strained look she always carried with her. Her husband and older son had both gone off to the Front, and she and the younger boy, Lucien, were left to take care of the farm. Her father, an old man past heavy labour, lived with them and did what he could to help. It was he who had taken the horse and cart to the fields as the sun was coming up.

"Café au lait, monsieur?"

She always offered him some, though she was not expected to provide food. He nodded and sat at the table. She placed the bowl in front of him.

"Pain et beurre, monsieur?"

He looked up. It was something special.

"Merci, madame," he said when she laid the thickly buttered bread on the table. He bit into it with obvious pleasure. She smiled briefly. He did the same, then pointed to the chair across from him. *"Madame, s'il vous plaît."*

She hesitated, but removed her apron from over her long skirts and sat down.

"Très bon." He drank more from the bowl and took another bite of the bread.

He found nothing more to say, but his look suggested he was pleased just to have her sit there. He was not uncomfortable, nor was she. She sat quietly for a long time, watching him as he ate.

"Les yeux sérieux, comme mon fils."

He smiled without knowing what she had said. He waited until he finished eating before speaking, and then it was only to thank her once more for the food. She took his bowl and walked to the stove, but he shook his head. He had never planned to sit for so long.

He left the house, shutting the door as quietly as he could behind him. The sun was not yet high enough in the sky to reach into the square enclosed by the house and barns. He looked across to where his men were billeted and saw no sign of anyone awake. He side-stepped the mud as best he could, going through the stone archway and onto the main road.

The regiment had rested in Louvencourt three times before. It was the favourite of all the French villages where the men had been sent between their tours in the trenches. It had not suffered the ravages of the artillery as had some others closer to the line. It had still some of the farming life it knew before the war, before the foreign troops crowded in and its road became rutted from the machinery of war passing through.

Hayward negotiated his way along the road. The day before he had detailed a work party to fill the worst of the mud holes. Together with the hold-up of rain, it made walking less of a messy affair than it had been most of the week. Farther along, the sun had risen above the rooftops and made the wetness glisten. Hayward removed his cap, despite the chill of the early morning, and let the sunlight pour onto his face.

He saw no one until the road turned to the right and he started uphill toward the church. Through an open door into a barn, he caught sight of Marie-Louise. She was in the gloom outside a stall, bending over a milk pail. She looked up, without surprise, then glanced at the farmhouse.

He walked slowly toward her. The light caught one side of her face and the curve of her neck. He glimpsed the tentative half-smile he had seen the first morning they had passed each other on the road.

It had taken several encounters after that before he had the courage to stop and speak to her. She had smiled at his awkward French, and nodded after he had finished, as if to thank him, then continued on her way. Their subsequent meetings led him to think back years, to the time he spent with girls in Topsail, where he went as a youth for summer camp with the Guards. They had been brief, formal affairs between blushing girls and hopelessly shy boys on Sunday afternoons when the people of the nearby con- gregations were invited to visit the campsites.

As he grew older he had not entirely over- come that shyness around young women, although he'd had daily dealings with many in the store where he worked. It was not a trait that looked good in the army, but neither was it one that often had any opportunity of showing itself. In Cairo, on the way to Gallipoli, when other officers sought out brothels, he made excuses, saying he would rather visit the pyramids again, which he did, though he got robbed of most of his money in the process.

Nearing Marie-Louise now, he was swept by the urge to embrace her. Yet, he stopped at a respectful distance, and held there, staring intently into her face. He knew her to be no more than sixteen.

She was unsure, unprepared for the seriousness of his look. He pleaded then with a smile, and looked away, and back again just as quickly.

He forgot the French he had memorized the night before and he kept quietly repeating *s'il vous plaît*, as if it were an expression of his affection for her. Suddenly he stepped forward and kissed her neck, in one motion almost, so quickly that she gasped.

She remained stiff and motionless, though she made no move to escape when he held her and drew her closer to him. He kissed her roughly on the mouth.

"Marie-Louise!" her mother called from the house. "Marie-Louise!"

Hayward held her still, and tried to speak. Gradually, his arms loosened.

She hurried away, only to discover she did not have the pail. He held it out to her.

"Allez, monsieur. J'ai beaucoup de travaux à faire. Vous ne pouvez venir ci tôt."

He watched her hurry to the house with the pail in her hand, glancing back at him several times.

Hayward slipped back to the street and wandered up the hill, unable to focus his mind on where he was going. A private from C Company passed by, smiling, and Hayward fumbled to acknowledge his salute. He walked more briskly now, trying to keep alert, given that others of the regiment were probably about.

Near the top of the hill he unbolted a gate and entered the churchyard. He had gone there many times before, although never so early in the day. The first time he was somewhat reluctant, having never been in a Catholic church. But he avoided looking for long at the statues and he kept to the back of the church, where he found the solitude he was seeking.

It was too early even for the frail young widow, wrapped in a black shawl and gripping her rosary beads, who came to mourn her husband killed at Ypres. Hayward crossed the stone floor to the last row of pews, indifferent to the chill and dankness of the place. He sat down with his head bowed slightly, one hand tight over the fist of the other. He closed his eyes, though not in prayer.

He and Marie-Louise together was all he could think about. He tried to fight back the exhilaration running through him still. All that held it in check was a nagging shame of having such thoughts in a house of God. There was some consolation in knowing he would never have gone in if the church had been Methodist.

Despite all, he felt an odd contentment. His breathing eased and there settled through him a satisfaction with himself he had not felt before. He loved her dearly. There could be no shame in that. He would come back to her when the fighting was over.

When he opened his eyes and looked up, it was on the cross that he tried to concentrate. He stared at it intently, to make a physical display of his faith. Only when he was satisfied that he had given his mind completely to God did he look away.

His eyes turned to the stained-glass window, the one with the young soldier of Christ in body armour, his hands holding the blade of a sword, the hilt before him like a cross. He was drawn to the picture almost against his will. The figure's melancholy had always unsettled him. Today he was determined he would overcome it.

Was it not God who willed that he unsheathe the sword? Was it not expected that he do battle against the ungodly? He recalled the sermons preached to them from the pulpits before they left the Island. The Empire was depending on its young men to halt the hordes of murderous Hun.

Long before any thought of war, the church had given them uniforms to wear as Methodist Guards. They had sharpened their skill with guns and paraded in the streets of St. John's on Empire Day. They were drilled by men who had fought the Boers.

The church door creaked open. Hayward watched the woman with the black shawl enter. She walked slowly to the front of the church, staring blankly into his face as she passed. She sat down, then shifted stiffly to her knees.

He could not look at her for long. He had witnessed death several times during his days as a soldier, but never had he known it through those whom it left at home. He stood, turned smartly and left the church.

TWO

Out in the sun, he briskly retraced his steps, slowing down as he passed the house of Marie-Louise. As he expected, she was not to be seen. He continued on, not wanting to arouse suspicion. Reveille had been at six, and more and more of the men were emerging from their sleeping quarters.

He turned into the farmyard where A Company's cookers were set up.

"Mornin', sir. Tea?"

He nodded. "Decent day, Williams."

"Finest kind. This'll be it for sure. Can't see 'em puttin' it off any longer."

"Men are getting anxious."

"We'll all be glad when it's over wit'," Williams

said, pouring the tea. "An' the men likes it 'ere, you know. Meself, I'd be happy to spend the rest o' the war right in this garden."

"The old lady Tilloloy would love that."

"She might be contrary, but she'll never be as contrary as a bullet up yer arse." Williams grinned and winked at him. "Idn't that right, sir?"

Williams took great pleasure in his relationship with the officers. He was at least a dozen years older than Hayward and a good many of those years he had spent as a cook on fishing schooners that sailed to the Labrador. He had told Hayward he had been in Ayre's and Sons, the Water Street store where Hayward had worked, when the schooners came into St. John's to sell their saltfish at the end of the season. Hayward couldn't, of course, recall seeing him there because there were so many men just like him, all looking for something fancy to bring back to their wives. Once he took back a metal contraption that riced potatoes, Williams had told him.

He returned to his work, ladling out cocoa to the line of sleep-rumpled men that formed behind the cooker. Williams had a comic line for most of them, usually glorifying the taste of the cocoa, which varied from morning to morning, depending on the last meal to be made in the cooker. They were the same comments he made every morning, and the men mumbled insults, the way they always did, about what the army had for them to live on.

A couple of the men from Hayward's platoon, Smith and Moss, wandered over to where he was standing. They lit cigarettes to kill the taste of the cocoa.

Smith was the oldest man in the platoon. He had a wife and two children. Moss was his buddy, nineteen and never out of Bonavista Bay until he joined up.

"Think the brass woulda give us a bit more of a lie-in this mornin', what, sir?" Smith said. "Las' night 'ere an' all."

Hayward smiled, affirming that they both knew there was no chance of that.

"After you left las' night, sir, the boys wouldn't shut up."

"Kept you awake, did they, Smith?"

"Then Bradley shows up wit' a bottle ..."

"T'ree parts full o' buckshee rum," Moss added in a half-whisper. He looked at Smith, uncertain whether he should have told, and relieved when Hayward didn't ask anything about it.

"Hard crew, what, sir? Don't know what to make of 'em meself."

Moss was about to inject something, but he held back. He took a long draw on his cigarette. "We got a civil day out of it."

"Yes, an' that we have," Smith said. "Nar draught o' wind. Great day on the saltwater." He laughed.

That got the two of them looking skyward. They were forever carrying on as if they were still fishermen back in Newfoundland.

"No trouble to jig a few today, eh, Mossie, ol' man?"

"We'll take Father's skiff an' anchor her off there be Mercer's Point."

Smith called over to the cook. "Williams, you got plenty o' fatback? Me and Mossie is takin' off out the bay to jig a few fish."

Williams brandished the ladle at him as if he were crazy.

"We wants you to have everything ready for a cook-up for when we gets back."

An explosion, louder than any heard all morning, roared in from their own front lines.

Their heads tightened into their shoulders.

"Bloody Hun got the wind up! Leave it to the likes o' that to spoil a good day's fishin'." Smith poured what was left of his cocoa onto the ground, and Moss did the same.

Hayward left them, smiling to himself as he walked back to the main road. A Company's Orderly Room was not far away. He took his time getting there, not anxious to set his day formally in motion.

He hung his hat on a nail near the door and joined the other officers. A cloud of smoke hung about them. They were intent on a map spread across a table in the centre of the room, the same map they had been studying for weeks. It detailed the Beaumont section of the Somme. On it had been drawn a thick network of red lines indicating the German trenches.

The captain spoke with his forefinger hovering over Hawthorn Ridge. "The mine goes tomorrow at 7:20."

"With zero hour at 7:30?" one of the officers asked.

The captain looked around the table and saw more questioning faces. Another spoke up. "Why the hell give them ten minutes to regroup, sir?"

"According to Headquarters there's forty thousand pounds of ammonal under that redoubt! Think Fritz is going to recover from a jolt like that in ten minutes?"

The question remained unanswered, as did a number of others. Generally, though, they had confidence in what the generals were telling them. The enemy had to be suffering badly from the massive amounts of artillery that had been pounding their lines day and night for a full week. General Haig had amassed an army that some said stretched for sixty miles. The Great Push could hardly fail.

Hayward left with Clarke, whose platoon was housed in a barn not far from that of his own men. They walked together to where they would all be assembling.

"Think the Germans know?"

"I'm sure of it. Good God, when I was on leave in London there were people in the streets who knew." Clarke spoke with a conviction Hayward could not ignore.

Over the past months the two had become friends even though in civilian life they would have been worlds apart. All Newfoundland knew of Clarke's grandfather, a wealthy businessman, who lived in a huge house on Circular Road in St. John's. Clarke had spent much of his life in England, where he had been sent to be educated. He rarely talked of his family, other than his brother, who was in the Royal Army Flying Corps.

Hayward and Clarke had both worked their way up the ranks from privates and had received their commissions within weeks of each other. It was in Gallipoli, surviving the flies and the Turkish snipers, that their friendship solidified. For Clarke, roughing it alongside men with backgrounds far less privileged than his own was proving his independence. Besides, he had said, he found more to like in them than in most people he had known at school in England.

"General de Lisle sounded pretty confident," Hayward said.

The divisional commander had addressed the regiment a few days before. He'd told them they need fear nothing, for the Allies had 263 battalions and the Hun but 32. And if all the gun ammunition were to be loaded on railway trucks, the line of trucks would go on for forty-six miles.

"We hope he got the damn figures right," Clarke said.

Hayward looked at him soberly.

Clarke brightened somewhat. "Allan, what can we expect to do but flatten the bastards."

The two smiled. Clarke rested his hand on Hayward's shoulder, feigning English sobriety. "Too long away from a woman can do this to a man, they say."

They walked in silence for the moment.

"What *did* your girl say?" Hayward knew that two days before an old family friend from London had visited Clarke and brought him several letters.

"She thinks of me whenever she passes Trafalgar Square," he said sprightly. "She finds the war terribly romantic."

"Have you told her how terribly fond of you the rats have become?"

He chuckled. "Hardly worth it, chum."

Hayward wanted to tell him about Marie-Louise, but knew he could not carry it off without an unseemly awkwardness showing through.

On another day they might have walked for some distance and not said much else, but this morning there was a desire to fill every second of their time together.

"Did you ever row in the Regatta?" Hayward

asked enthusiastically.

"No. I rowed at school in England. Steele has, I'd say."

"He won the city walking race in '13."

"Fine athlete, Steele."

"We could make up a team when we get back to St. John's, when it's over. What do you say to that? Wilf and the captain, they'd give it a go."

"We could call ourselves the Regimental A's, don't you think?"

"And give those fishermen from Outer Cove a bloody good run for the money."

"And win the blasted heart of every sweet young thing on shore!"

Their voices raced ahead of them, turning a few heads as they rounded the corner to where the company had fallen in. The corporals buried self-satisfied smiles, all the time watching the captain's eyes follow Clarke and Hayward to their places.

The company sergeant-major snapped the men to attention. "Fix bayonets! Rear rank, one pace step back. March! Rear rank, right. Dress!"

The captain made a slow walk down the line, stopping occasionally for a closer look at a

man's uniform. Where he found something not
to his liking he made a quick comment and
pressed on, knowing that at this point there
were concerns greater than minor infractions of
dress. The appearance of one man warranted
closer attention.

"Something in your stomach that wants to
come up, Pendergast?"

"No, sir."

"Not used to the wine are you, Private?"

"No, sir."

"Think you can hold that look for the enemy?"

"Yes, sir."

The captain nodded to the sergeant-major.

"Unfix bayonets!" the sergeant-major yelled,
almost directly into Pendergast's ear.

The private's grimace deepened.

"Even better, Private."

"Port arms!" bellowed the sergeant-major.

The captain proceeded with the inspection
of arms, walking more slowly this time, taking
considerable care to see that their Lee-Enfields
had been thoroughly cleaned and were ready for
use. As he moved down the line the men he
passed lowered their rifles, rested the butts on
the ground by their sides and stood at ease. The

captain found little to complain about.

He stood ready to address the company. The sergeant-major called them to attention and gave the order to close ranks.

"We move to the line at 9 o'clock tonight." The captain's voice, loud and solemn, attempted to give weight to something they had known for several days. He looked up and down the line. "Today we spend in final preparation for that move. Do what you have to do to get your billets and yourselves in order. The remainder of the day is yours. I suggest you get some rest. It's going to be a long night, and a longer day tomorrow."

The men were dismissed and started to move off, with more hesitation than was usual for early in the morning. They bunched together and grew louder and more animated with the exchange of stories about the night before. There was little effort to keep any of it from being overheard by the officers, who were themselves standing together and running on about the late-night antics of a lieutenant in another company.

Hayward and Clarke left, and were joined by Wilf Myers, another second lieutenant in A Company, as they headed to the mess for breakfast. Myers reacted with indifference when Hayward brought up the idea of putting together a rowing team for the Regatta.

"Think about it," Hayward said, knowing better than to press him on the matter.

They walked on in silence, except to curse the trouble it was taking to avoid the mud, until Clarke could handle it no longer and started into a song they'd been belting out the night before over some sour French beer.

> "I have no pain, dear mother, now,
> But oh, I am so dry!
> Connect me to a brewery
> And leave me there to die."

"What have you got to be so bloody cheerful about?" Myers snapped.

Clarke glanced at Hayward, raising his eyebrows. He took out a dented silver case and removed a cigarette. He tapped the end of the cigarette against the case.

"Think there'll be anything to sing about tomorrow?" Myers barked at him.

Clarke lit his cigarette. "I know a rousing hymn or two." He started to sing, to the tune of

"Take It to the Lord in Prayer." Myers walked off ahead of them.

> "When this bloody war is over
> Oh, how happy I shall be …"

Clarke dragged out the last line and stopped. "Righto, old chum. Steady on."

Myers halted, and faced them both.

"It's our bloody hides, too," Hayward snapped before he had a chance to speak.

Clarke put it to him. "So, do you want to dig the holes for us before we go? I can put my hands on a bleedin' shovel."

Hayward could see it getting out of hand. "We're in this together. It can't be any worse than the mess we've gone through already."

"What do you bloody well want, Wilf — jam on it?" Clarke sang out. His laughter filled the street.

Myers smiled stiffly. He said nothing the rest of the way. After a while Clarke started to hum, a tune that Hayward didn't know, one he had been humming since he came back from leave in London.

THREE

When they arrived at the company mess, the kitchen of a house where some officers were billeted, they were met with the smell of eggs frying. Eggs, though not a rarity, still had a slightly exotic quality for men gone thin on too many meals of bully beef. But it was the sight of an open jar of jam, strawberry and not the infernal apple and plum, that caused greater excitement.

"Captain's treat," the cook explained. "Brought back three bottles from Blighty on his last leave. Said he's been saving it for the right occasion."

"The right occasion," Clarke said. "Tell the man he has our undying gratitude."

"And a young lady came by with some bread." The cook paused, then added with a grin, "for *m'sieur l'officer 'Ayward.*"

The kitchen erupted with shouts of derision. "Obviously," someone declared, "the gentleman has something we haven't got."

"Or more of something we have," Clarke shouted, holding up the loaf.

Hayward, red-faced, sat at the table and tried to ignore them. He tore a piece from the loaf and smothered it with jam in a vain attempt at being comic.

He was the butt of their ribald jokes throughout the meal. There was some satisfaction to be had from his sudden reputation as a randy young man, and in time he was able to leave the table without it appearing that he was doing so out of embarrassment. Yet he hadn't really been able to enjoy the food, exceptional though it was.

He returned to his billet at Madame Cornot's. She had gone to the fields and the place was empty except for eight-year-old Lucien, who'd been left to attend to the animals. He was racing around noisily in his *sabots*, chasing a frazzled chicken that had escaped from its pen.

Lucien rarely looked anything but dirty, in his collarless shirt and threadbare shorts. His legs were meant to be covered by the long stockings that were forever around his ankles.

The men housed in the barn rarely used his name, but referred to him instead as "the young gaffer". They were constantly putting him up to no good, for which he received severe reprimands from his mother. On more than one occasion Hayward had come to his defence and attempted to explain to the boy's mother the cause of his misbehaviour. Lucien had taken a strong liking to Hayward for that reason and followed him about constantly.

With Hayward's help Lucien managed to corner the bird. He tossed it squawking back into the pen, spitting words at it similar to those his mother used on him.

When Hayward went in the house and up the stairs to the room where he slept, Lucien was behind him, slowly and deliberately repeating some English words Hayward had taught him the day before. The boy had been the one to teach Hayward what French he used, and they often engaged in a game in which one of them would point to an object and the other had to come up with the word for it in the foreign language.

This morning Hayward did not respond, and Lucien's disappointment was obvious. He hung by the door and watched his friend gather up all his belongings and spread them out on the bed. Hayward opened a valise and began to fold some of the clothes and place them carefully inside. The valise was half full before he looked up at the boy still standing there.

Lucien smiled. Hayward sat on the bed and motioned for the boy to sit next to him. He withdrew his Mk VI pistol from its leather pouch and after checking that it wasn't loaded, held it out in front of the boy.

The gun had been the object of Lucien's curiosity for as long as the two had known each other. Hayward had permitted him to hold it only once before, and then for just a few seconds. Lucien drew his head back in disbelief when Hayward passed him the pistol and nodded for him to examine it.

Its weight alone was enough to widen the eyes of a boy used to playing with guns made from broken tree limbs. He turned it over in his hands, staring at it all the while. He ran his fingers along the black metal barrel, and over the hammer, stopping finally at the smooth curve of the trigger.

Hayward nodded again. Lucien gripped the gun as best he could and raised it off his other hand, his forefinger just long enough to touch the trigger. The gun was too heavy and unfamiliar for him, but he extended his arm as if he was taking aim. He jerked his arm and let out a sound that mimicked a pistol shot.

"Tu aurais tué beaucoup de Boches." Lucien said with an eagerness that Hayward found difficult to ignore.

After a few moments Hayward took the gun and put it back in its leather case. The boy watched him intently, until they heard the noise outside of the men returning from breakfast. Hayward made his way downstairs.

The barn was just big enough to accommodate the platoon. It was dim and smelly, but the straw was dry and the farm animals were kept in a separate building, which is more than could be said of other places they'd slept. Each of the men had worked out a space of his own and did what he could to make it livable. Their gear hung on nails in a near orderly fashion, and some had pinned up pictures, of ocean scenes sent from home, or the tamer of the smutty postcards bought in the backstreets of Cairo and Rouen.

A good half of the men had been together since before Hayward had taken charge of them, and from time to time more had been added to replace those assigned to other units such as the signals corps or the Lewis gunners. He had lost only one man in action, and that was the result of a stray bullet catching the fellow in the shoulder. He was in England now, recovering nicely according to his letter, but with no chance of reassignment in time for the Great Push.

They were a good lot. There were the usual gripes about food and the trench-digging duties, and the strain of endless training exercises had worn some tempers thin. But for the most part they had kept their humour through it all.

A good many of them had been used to rigorous outdoor work before they joined up, and their time in the regiment had only toughened them further. What they lacked in military precision they more than made up for in their willingness to do whatever was asked of them. A good trait, and one the colonel had come to appreciate.

Inside the barn, Hayward beckoned to one of the corporals. The fellow had received his second chevron and been posted to the section only a week before. His predecessor, now a sergeant assigned to the quartermaster, had been well liked, and Hayward knew Bennett was having some difficulty being accepted by the men. Smith, especially, was giving him a hard time.

"No problems?"

"No problems."

"How's Murphy's hand?"

"Says he's fine, sir. Says he's not going to the M.O. Don't want to take any chances on missing the show."

"Pendergast?"

"Pitiful, sir. Serves him right."

Hayward smiled. "He'll sleep it off this afternoon."

Smith came up to them, intent, Hayward could tell from the look in his eye, on stirring up something.

"Did the corporal pass along our request, sir?" He rubbed his jaw with the back of his hand.

"What request, Smith?" Bennett snapped.

"The football match. We want Mr. Hayward

to make C Company an offer."

"What are you goin' on about?" said Bennett.

"Mr. Hayward, the boys wants a little wager. Whoever loses gets the other company's rum ration before we go over the top."

The corporal glared at him. "Smith, you know bloody well that's against regulations."

"Is it, sir?" He turned to Hayward. "I wasn't sure."

"Now you're sure." Hayward knew better than to become part of his little game. "Do the corporal a favour and round up the men."

"Of course, sir." Smith went off, smiling broadly.

"The man's a useless idiot," Bennett said.

Hayward thought of telling him about the job Smith did on a couple of Turks. He didn't say anything, which, he could see, didn't go over too well with the corporal.

The men gathered together—a hardened lot, bare headed, no two alike in the way they stood there, tunics hanging open, sharing draws on their cigarettes. They smiled at nothing in particular.

"I s'pose breakfast was no worse than normal?" Hayward said.

"Better, sir. Bacon, 'nough to feed a bleedin' army, what."

"We was figurin' on the Kaiser sendin' over some sausages."

"Ah, he can keep 'em," another piped up. "Fatten theirselves up 'fore the kill."

Hayward quickly ran through the orders for the day. "This place is to be left perfectly clean," he added, "and that means better than we found it."

Bennett spoke up. "I've already made it clear to the men, sir, that if you're not satisfied, sir, not to expect much rest this afternoon." Hayward could see the men didn't appreciate the interjection, even less the tone of voice.

"The lance corporals will supervise the storage of kits in the QM stores at 1:30. I'll make a personal inspection at 2 o'clock, and after that the footballers will have their crack at C Company."

There was a stiff cheer, over which someone shouted, "You lot from the Sout' Coast, don't let that St. John's crowd score all the ruddy goals this time."

"Questions?"

When the noise died down there was only one. "Sir, is the colonel sweatin' it, sir?"

"The colonel is calmer than what you are."

It was what they wanted to hear and, as Hayward left and the men dispersed, there was only a quiet rumble of voices, precisely what Hayward was hoping for.

He ran into Clarke outside the barn. Clarke looked at him with mock seriousness, a remnant of his smirk from the breakfast table showing through. "My amorous friend," he said, putting a hand on his shoulder, "the captain would like to have a few words with you regarding some affair. A military one, I presume."

Hayward kept a straight face. He spoke in a low, scornful voice. "Clarke, you're a proper ass." He smiled jovially and walked off.

Clarke was lost for words for the moment. Then he called out, "The Methodist lad is back-sliding!"

Hayward was rather pleased to walk away thinking that Clarke didn't have him figured out completely.

FOUR

The morning sun had dried the road considerably, and for the first time in several days he could walk it without having to keep his mind on avoiding the mud. His pace picked up and he began to hum loudly. He didn't rightly know what to make of this sudden exhilaration. He knew it odd, but he was equally conscious of the urge to let it race through him unchecked.

He was heading to the Orderly Room to report to the captain, but stopped abruptly and turned in the direction of Marie-Louise's house. This change of will, near defiance in his mind, quickened his blood even more. His stride became uneven, his thoughts scattered, until he knew it couldn't continue.

He would have to slow down and let his head settle. With routine briskness he acknowledged several men walking by. He sharpened his stare, keen to restore a sense of efficiency.

As he drew nearer to Marie-Louise's any anxiety about what he would say or do passed. There was only the realization that he had to make the effort, that the time for making it would soon be gone. He would not leave Louvencourt again with regrets.

He entered the enclosure where she lived. The house and barns were modest structures, made mostly of mortar plastered over wood framing, and were in great need of repair. There was only Marie-Louise and her mother, and their time was taken with the animals and with making bread to sell to the troops.

The aroma of freshly baked bread hung in the air, and for a moment Hayward stood and breathed it deeply. He recalled his mother's bread, and how he would cut it still warm and spread it with molasses. Almost for relief, he walked to the door of the house.

It was wide open. Heat drifted across his face like gauze, narrowing his eyes and causing him to lose his breath for a moment. He could see a pile of long loaves leaning against a table, with several round ones stacked on top of it. He knocked quietly against the door-frame and stood back, recovering his breath.

He had not seen Marie-Louise's mother close up before. She was a small woman, with a face dark and creased, though not as stern as he'd imagined. She smiled broadly at him as she wiped the sweat from her forehead with the end of her apron. Despite the heat, she was wearing the heavy layers of clothing and the close-fitting bonnet common to many women of the village.

She did not appear surprised at his being there. She sputtered out something he had no chance of understanding, at the same time motioning to a part of the room he could not see.

"Pardon, madame?" His words were weaker and sounded less like French than he had hoped.

Marie-Louise came quietly into view. With her hand to her face in embarrassment, she stood behind her mother.

The mother said something and chuckled. Hayward laughed along with her.

"Pain, madame," he said, with great enthusiasm. *"Merci."* He nodded and pointed to the table behind them.

She scurried inside, calling back to him, *"Combien?* One? Two? *Trois, monsieur?"*

He looked to Marie-Louise for help, but when she did not intercede, he realized she had not told her mother about the loaf she'd brought to the company mess.

"One," he mumbled, and began searching his pocket for centimes.

She handed the bread to him. He paid her a little more than it cost, and she stood back and smiled, in the same way she had done when she first came to the door. It remained for him only to leave. He caught Marie-Louise's eye and raised his free hand slightly to her. He knew anything private between them would have to wait.

He glanced back only once and saw the mother standing in the doorway, still smiling. On he went, as casually as he could. The long loaf hung like an appendage by his side.

His walk back was a manoeuvre to avoid at all costs encountering any of the officers with whom he had shared breakfast. When one of them appeared in the distance he quickly turned onto a lane between two houses and skirted several vegetable gardens before making it back to the main road, his boots coated with mud and manure.

Farther on, his fortune changed. He spotted Lucien idly following a dog. The boy came running when he called to him. Hayward quickly handed over the loaf, with a few words in French that he hoped would get the bread to his room and, with luck, under his bed.

He walked on, feeling less foolish, working the stiffness out of his stride. He approached the Orderly Room anxious to get on with whatever the captain had in mind for him to do.

The Orderly Room was surprisingly quiet. On days previous there was certain to be a steady flow of officers seeking clarification of orders and a place to have a smoke in comfort. Now, the intermittent clatter of a typewriter in need of repair and the grumbling of the man trying to use it were the only disturbances. The captain sat studying the map that had been the focus of discussion earlier in the morning. Not until he looked up did Hayward salute and approach him.

"Heard from your mother recently, Allan?"

Hayward had not expected anything so personal. "Yes, sir. Last week," he replied, rather lamely. His mother and the captain's aunt were close friends and members of the same church committees. "She's sending a photograph of the new church. It was dedicated on the eighteenth, you know."

"Aunt Gladys said it's very fine, Byzantine style, she said. There'll be nothing like it in St. John's."

The Cochrane Street church had burnt to the ground during a freezing-rain storm on a Sunday evening in the January before the war. It was something Hayward and the captain had talked over many times, speculating on the cause. Neither of them had been attending the service during which the fire had started, but they both rushed to the scene once the word was out and stood together in disbelief with others of the Methodist Guards.

The captain had been a leader in the Guards, and his relationship with Hayward went back many years. Hayward was sure he had been instrumental in his getting a commission, though the captain had never said anything to suggest it, nor anything that indicated whether Hayward was living up to his expectations. The captain rarely took him into his confidence, as he did some others, and there remained an unspoken wall between them that on some days left Hayward wondering what was being said about him to the higher ranks.

It came then as a surprise that the captain now assigned him the task of going to the colonel and checking on the matter of the draft of new men due from the base camp at Rouen sometime that day. Hayward's response was not without a hint of his satisfaction at being singled out for the task. If the truth were known, Hayward reasoned, it might also be the captain's way of bringing him more to the attention of the colonel.

"Tell me, Allan, what's for you after the war?"

Hayward had expected him to get straight to the details of the assignment. And it was not that he hadn't given the question serious thought; it was more the impatient tone in which it was asked that caused him to stumble slightly. "I expect … I'll go back to my old position."

"You're worthy of more than a store clerk's job, old man."

"Mr. Ayre has always treated me well." He regretted that it sounded like a defence.

"You'll be going back an officer. You should take advantage of that."

"I hadn't thought we'd be treated too differently."

"To some we'll be heroes, I suspect. There will no doubt be business opportunities, and marriage opportunities."

That had never occurred to Hayward. He was at a loss for a response.

Eventually the captain put him at ease. "If the colonel is not there, see what you can find out from whoever is about. I would like a reply within the half hour, unless you have more urgent matters to attend to."

"No, there's nothing."

There remained with him all the way to Headquarters the notion that he would have to sharpen his opinions and give a better account of himself if he hoped to ever get beyond the rank of second lieutenant.

Regiment Headquarters, whatever premises it occupied, had about it a strong sense of the colonel. It was the air of efficiency, as it was the smell of the dubbin regularly applied to his riding gear. As Hayward entered, the colonel was discussing something intently with his adjutant.

"See to it that transport is aware of this." He was about to turn his attention to other matters when he noticed Hayward. "Yes?"

Hayward stepped forward and saluted. "The captain was wondering about the new draft of men, sir. He would like to know if you have any new information, sir."

The colonel picked up a pen and began to write in a leather-bound notebook. "Tell him no." He hadn't bothered to look up.

Hayward waited for something more, though he could see the colonel was now otherwise occupied. He saluted and began to leave.

"Sometime this afternoon," the colonel said. Hayward was almost out the door. He turned around. "And Hayward, your men, how are they?"

"Fine, sir."

"It might not be easy."

"You can count on them."

"I knew I could."

"Yes, sir."

"Very good, Hayward." The colonel stared at him for a moment and then went back to his writing.

Hayward was outside again without being sure if he had found out all he needed to know. The colonel had never been an easy man to deal with when he had other things on his mind.

There was a certain distance to be kept, except when he himself was of a mind to narrow it. Some said it was because he was an Englishman in charge of a regiment of colonials and that it was a natural thing. Others, Clarke included, were not so kind, especially after the training exercises, when the colonel had severely reprimanded the men for not being up to scratch. And none of them would soon forget the fourteen-mile march he forced on them in the heat of the Egyptian desert.

During the months leading to the Great Push, though, the men had proved themselves tougher than most, and the colonel had finally told them so. They had gained his respect and they were determined to keep it. Their loyalty to England and its army men was as strong as it had ever been.

On his way back to the Orderly Room, Hayward dwelt on just how quickly the men accepted what the colonel and the generals were now asking of them. If there was any aggravation, most were keeping it to themselves. The few that did voice it were letting down the regiment as far as Hayward was concerned. If there was one thing he prided himself on, it was his steadfastness when the going was rough.

The captain took his report without much comment other than to inquire off-handedly as to the colonel's general mood at the moment.

"Civil enough." Hayward added, "From what I can tell. You know the colonel."

"Yes."

The colonel had been at it long enough to know what he was about, certainly. And they both knew he was following orders, just as they were. It was his job to get the men prepared, and as far as Hayward could tell the men were as ready as ever they'd be.

"The anticipation is the worst of it," the captain said.

Hayward left the captain still studying the situation maps. For the first time since the battle plan was revealed Hayward found himself pondering what there might be about the next day that was being kept from them. It was taken for granted that they were never given the full picture, only as much as they needed to know to carry out their part in it. And there was, of course, a lot that nobody could know until the attack actually began. Still, he couldn't help feeling that the expectations of a few days before had somehow changed. The prediction of a grand success certainly wasn't being heard with the same frequency nor pronounced with the same authority.

FIVE

He needed some time alone. That was one thing about army life that he had never been able to get used to—the unending contact with others at close quarters.

He walked the road that led out of the village to the northwest, toward Vauchelles-les-Authie. Several transport vehicles from another regiment laboured past him, wheels encrusted with mud.

"How goes it?" one of the drivers shouted to him.

"Thumbs up, chum," Hayward called back out of habit.

When he had gone far enough that no one from the village could possibly see him, he took a narrow foot path that ran between two farmers' fields. Along it he looked for a place that was reasonably dry. When he found one he loosened his tunic and sat down, resting his arms on his knees.

In the distance were the fields the battalions had trampled in practising their manoeuvres. Time and time again, under the scrutiny of the brigadier-general, they had simulated the attack as it would take place on the Great Day. The whole show had been planned in relentless detail. Every soldier knew precisely what was expected of him.

Hayward found it impossible to clear his mind of it, but he was able for the moment to think of it still as part of some great adventure. The Blue Puttees they were called when they left Newfoundland two years before. Their puttees were a blue flannel because there was no khaki material to be had when their uniforms were made. Those puttees had long since been replaced, while the men trained in Scotland, and Hayward had sent his back home to have as a keepsake when he returned.

It was great fun, those early days. Some said the war would be over by Christmas and they would miss out. At the most it would last a year.

When the first man was killed, McWhirter it was, at Suvla Bay, they each knew it could have been any one of them, and from that day on it became less of an adventure.

Still, Hayward knew, he could never have held back when most all the boys in the Guards were joining up. He was no slacker. He had made his way to the Armoury on Harvey Road and volunteered the day after forty members of the Catholic Cadet Corps signed up in a single group. By the second week of September they were all under canvas and on October 4 they marched past cheering crowds through the streets of St. John's and boarded the *Florizel*.

Of the countries he had sailed to after his training, only now, for France, did he feel much attraction. The grain rippling with the wind made him think of the lakes where he went as a boy to fish. The colours were stronger, especially the red of the wild poppies along the roadside, but the solitude was the same. He had come to fields such as this when they first arrived, with thick flakes of snow flying in the air, and he was reminded of the times he had gone with his uncle across the Topsail barrens to hunt partridge.

Even now, with concentration, he could ignore the artillery, as the villagers did. From his tunic pocket he took a pen and the paper he had been saving explicitly for writing a letter home. He unfolded the paper and placed it against his field notebook. He rubbed out the creases as best he could, then in neat, handsome script, he began.

June 30, 1916   *France*

Dear Mother and Father,

I have been thinking today of what it will be that you will find most different about me when I return. Despite the food here, look for someone who fills more of your doorway, and not the "rake" that Father called me before I left home.

No moustache, though many of the other officers have them now. I made the attempt, as I told you before, but it would not grow to a thickness to match any of theirs so I recently did away with it. Tell Father his supply of wax was premature. I shared it out among several of the new lance jacks.

I think you will find me different in out-

look. I have seen much beyond the shores of Newfoundland and should think I will bring back remembrances of places most people on our fair Island know nothing about.

Still, I shall be very glad to be home. Nothing would do my heart better than to see you and Amy. And then to walk along Monkstown Road to visit Uncle Harold (is he still as talkative as ever?) and perhaps to the Nickel to take in a moving picture with some of the old school chums.

Tonight we head to the front lines again. I wish I could tell you what tomorrow will bring, but we cannot take any chances on information getting into the wrong hands. Enough to say that there has been nothing to match it so far. The Hun will be too stunned to know what hit them. No doubt you will be reading about it in The Daily News.

Don't worry about my safety. I am in charge of a good bunch of men and we all know what we are about. If one or two are wounded then that is all that can be done. It means they'll be home all the quicker.

Remember me to Amy. She is a young lady now, I know. Tell her that her brother will buy her the most wonderful perfume he can find the next time he is on leave.

Your loving son,
Allan

He folded the letter along the same creases and placed it in an envelope taken from the pocket of his tunic.

He checked his watch. He loosened his tie, undid the top button of his shirt and walked a few steps to take a leak.

Then he spread out his tunic and lay on his back. He was feeling like a truant schoolboy.

Bright blue sky stretched forever above him, completely filling his field of vision except for the stalks of winter wheat skirting the edges. He held up an arm to shield the sun from his eyes and stared at the few clouds and the way they drifted aimlessly across the sky.

He grew dazed by a view that was completely free of anything to do with the war. It was as if he had set himself fearlessly adrift. Gradually, there surfaced desires he had long ago learned to force away. Thoughts of Marie-Louise weaved about in his head.

His arms stretched out to each side of him, rigid and sinewy. His fists tightened into knots.

That tension held, his eyes wide open, until he felt he would burst. Then overhead, the whine of an aeroplane snapped it and he slumped back.

He sat up quickly and, shielding his eyes from the sun again, he tried to see whether it was an enemy plane. It was rather far away, but given its erratic flying pattern, he decided it had to be a Fokker on reconnaissance. Ground fire could be heard from gun positions close to the Front, but the plane dodged it and escaped back into German territory.

It was all too strong a reminder of who he was and where he was expected to be. He brushed off his coat and, though it was wet, he put it on, hoping the sun would have it dry by the time he was back.

His walk was slower, calculated to take as long as possible without it appearing that he was reluctant to go back. He stopped once—to look at a pair of birds skittering through the branches of a tree. He wondered what species they were. Not that it mattered, he thought after he gave up looking and walked on, though it would have been good to know.

SIX

He found the village alive with men. He assumed they had packed away their personal possessions and were left with little to do other than wait for the next meal and for the *estaminets* to open so they could have a few drinks.

As he turned into his billet he came face to face with Clarke.

"Ah, the estranged young officer! Don't tell me—the captain made you come clean about your various romantic intrigues and it took forever."

Hayward ignored the remark, and Clarke took this as a challenge. He followed Hayward into the house.

"Your secret is safe with me, chum." He was a few steps behind Hayward as they ascended the stairs. "The skirt with the bread, she's not the only one, I can tell. You were at it in Bonneville and Englebelmer. You'll have half the young things this side of the Somme pushing prams before the year is out."

Hayward wasn't about to let the fellow get to him.

"Out of the house and it's hardly daylight— nothing like it. Hot stuff, fresh from the oven. She got a sister?"

"If she did, she wouldn't be giving you a second look."

Clarke's words took on a new vigour. "Leave me to pick up the crumbs, what?"

"Clarke, do you have to be such a bloody pain?"

"*Le pain, monsieur. Aimez-vous le pain?*"

Clarke pulled out from under Hayward's bed the loaf Lucien had put there and held it out like a sword. "Ah! Defend yourself, *monsieur!* Man cannot live by *pain* alone!"

Startled, Hayward stumbled back and fell onto the bed. Clarke waved the loaf about with a grand flourish and jabbed it into his friend's chest. Hayward grabbed at it and the bread broke in two, sending him smack against the wall.

They fell about laughing then, like a pair of boys revelling in a foolish prank. They laughed so hard they doubled over, their arms pressed against their chests. When, finally, they had exhausted the fun of it, they sat back on the beds and chewed hunks of the bread and talked about how damn much they missed home.

It was noise from the barn that eventually brought them to their feet. They went outside, following the blaring voice of Corporal Bennett. Just inside the barn door they found him, stiff and red faced, standing in front of Private Moss.

"You're a fool, Moss. If you weren't, you'd keep your mouth shut and do what you're told! You're not home on the wharf with the boys now."

The corporal had not seen the two officers approach. He eased himself away from Moss. "Disobeying an order, sir. Harvey and Moss here were assigned to carry a trench bridge when we go over the top tomorrow, sir. For some reason he thinks it should be him and Smith."

"Me and Smit' is buddies, sir. We been together ever since I finished training."

"Buddies, is it?" Bennett said scornfully. "A pair of bloody nuisances is what I'd call it."

Hayward could see that Moss was on the

brink of snapping back with something that could only make it worse for him. "I'd say Private Moss needs to be set straight on this," he said, his superior rank clear to them both. "Moss, you come with me."

Hayward left the corporal to vent his anger in Clarke's direction. He offered Clarke a wry grin.

Clarke sent a glowering look his way, then turned to Bennett with exaggerated sympathy. "I've always said you corporals have the worst bloody job in the army."

Hayward led Moss to a corner of the yard where no one would hear them.

"You're a hard nut. You can't be smart-mouthin' the corporal and getting away with it. I should be running you for this."

Moss stood brooding, hardly looking at Hayward. There was a bullheadedness still in him that would have been knocked out of most men after their first few months in uniform.

"What did you say to him?"

"He got it in for Smit' an' me. When we goes over, we're goin' over together."

"I won't say no."

Moss looked at him squarely.

"When the time comes, Moss."

His gloom showed some sign of breaking.

"This is between me and you and Smith. And stay out of the corporal's way, the both of you."

"Yes, sir. Thank you." He was suddenly looking brighter. "Sir, I only told 'en he was too big in hesself."

"I was wondering."

"And he is, too. What's he goin' to be like atall, if he ever gets another stripe on hes sleeve?"

Hayward had to force away a smile and the temptation to give him a good-natured smack on the back.

When the other two emerged from the barn, Hayward quickly made it clear there'd be nothing more to worry about from Moss. The obstinate young private went past without a glance at Bennett.

"They've done a good job of it," Hayward said, diverting the corporal's attention to the matter of the barn clean-up.

"I had a look. It's a swell job." Clarke added, with a seriousness that only Hayward could see through, "I was just saying he'll be telling *us* what to do before the war is out. The man's not slack when it comes to getting things done. Are you, Corporal?"

"I do my best, sir."

"That's the ticket, old man. Captain has his eye on you. Wouldn't you say, Mr. Hayward?"

"No doubt."

They left Bennett not knowing what to do with himself.

"Moss is right," Hayward said. "Another stripe and he'll be the proper jackass."

They were about to go back in the house when Lucien ran into them on his way out the door.

"Whoa!" Clarke grabbed him around the waist and flipped him roughly over in the air before planting his feet back on the ground.

"*Monsieur Hayward,*" said Lucien, as if nothing had happened to him. "*Venez avec moi! Venez avec moi!*"

Hayward looked at Clarke.

"Go on."

"*Vite! Vite!*"

"Who knows what the devil he's been up to."

Hayward followed him around the side of the barn, past the stench of the latrines (and the painful salute of Pendergast, who was standing outside), through the vegetable garden, and eventually to a decaying, windowless shed, half hidden by thorny bushes. Hayward knew it only as the place where some of the men would congregate on paydays to play crown and anchor.

Lucien had jolted to a stop just outside the door and now stood there stiffly, motioning with a slight twist of his head for Hayward to go inside.

Perplexed, Hayward stared at the boy, then pulled open the door.

There was Marie-Louise. He could hardly believe it. She glanced at him, and for a moment there was a look of relief on her face.

Hayward turned to Lucien, who was grinning broadly, and motioned for the boy to go away. He did, reluctantly, and not before he poked his head inside and received assurance from Marie-Louise that he wasn't needed any more.

Hayward waited outside until he saw the last of Lucien in the distance, although as he stepped past the door he was sure he heard him laugh and shout an obscenity in English.

He quietly approached Marie-Louise. Her cheeks were wet. He took hold of her head and turned it toward him.

"*Tu vas partir ce soir?*" she said.

At first he had no idea what it meant. It was only when she pressed into his hand a photograph—a small, oval one of her on the steps of the cathedral in Amiens—that he realized what it might be that she had said and why she had been crying.

He held her tightly. He could feel her body trembling. "No tears," he said, and with muted words he tried to soothe her. His kiss brushed her neck as he drew back, looking into her eyes. "A few days only."

He pressed his lips firmly against hers. His arms tightened around her waist. He pressed her roughly against the closed door, through him rose an intense need for her that he didn't care if he held back.

Her tears returned. "No," she said. She pushed at him and finally, when her crying broke through to him, he let her go.

Abruptly, he drew back, embarrassed. He searched for a way to show his regret, but could only stare at her despondently, sputtering words she had no way of understanding.

Her crying subsided, but by then he had gone. She was left standing in the doorway. He was out of her sight before he stopped and looked back through the branches of the trees. She seemed about to call his name, but did not, as

if afraid it would draw attention to herself. He
watched her disappear along the path.

SEVEN

During the noon-hour meal he did what he could to look normal. Clarke jabbed at him with the details he had managed to get out of the boy. Hayward denied it all.

Fortunately, the others had plenty more to concern them. When the captain joined them partway through the meal he came with news that the draft of new men was expected within the hour. It brought a mixture of anticipation at there being among the lot someone known to them, and misgivings about how well any of them would fit in with but a few hours before the march to the Front.

"Send them all for a tramp over the top ahead of us."

"There's nothin' like a good taste o' Boche to bring the poor sots to their senses."

"We'll need every one of these men, and more if we could get them," the captain said, sounding the mandatory note of caution.

"That we will, sir. And prime lads, too, every one of them," someone added, rather less seriously.

"I've got two trench ladders to reassign. I hope there's a few of them from the lumberwoods."

"A St. John's lad won't do? Is that what you're saying?"

"Fresh from the Methodist College. Smacking his knuckles at the St. Bon's boys all his life."

"A born loser, then," quipped someone at the far end of the table.

"Now chaps," the captain interjected, "let's not bring religion into it."

There was a lull in the conversation and a few measured glances about the table. Hayward knew there was not one of them who wasn't now thinking about the heated controversy that had arisen back in Newfoundland over the fact that more Protestants than Catholics had received commissions as officers in the regiment.

"Good God," said Clarke, "we all know how

well the Hun bullets can discriminate between us dirty black Protestants and you micks."

The captain cracked a smile, and laughter spread down both sides of the table.

When it died away it was the voice of the cook that could be heard above them all. "Any more for any more?"

"More bully stew? Not I. I'll save my stomach for the big one tonight."

"The last supper, is it?"

"Ah, a soirée!"

"No, boys, a great scoff 'fore the Great Push."

"Righto, righto."

A solid cheer rose up for the cook. Most of them took it as a good note on which to break up the meal. As Hayward hoped, Clarke had things to be doing and eventually left in animated conversation with some others.

Hayward poured himself a second cup of tea and sat back at the table. He would have preferred the time to himself, but Myers lingered behind, eventually sitting in the chair next to him.

Hayward was surprised. Myers's exterior had always been stiffer than that of most his rank and he had never been one to initiate small talk. Hayward lit a cigarette without intending to and rearranged himself in his chair.

It was common opinion among the other officers that Myers was hardly meant for the army and was in it because of his cousin, a captain in charge of one of the regiment's other companies. He was not long back from leave, extended, rumour had it, because of an incident in which he lost control in front of his men. On his return Myers had been reassigned to A Company, with duties at Regiment Headquarters when the colonel had need of him.

"I'll do it," he said earnestly. "I want to. We'll make up a team and we can win. I'm sure of it."

Hayward looked at him, puzzled.

"My uncle's shell, *The Blue Mist* ... with the right crew, there's nothing in St. John's can touch her. We'd have to train hard to get the stroke down, but we can do it."

Only then did he realize what Myers was talking about.

"You can be darn sure the other companies will want to have teams, too. We can make it a regiment race. It'll be a devil of a show for the crowd back home."

"You're sure you'd want to do it, Wilf?"

"When this war is over there's a lot I'm going to do. I get through this, and I'm laughin'. My chances are good. An officer's chances are better, aren't they, than a regular chap's? They said I was one of the best in training."

It bothered Hayward how Myers kept looking to the other side of the room as he talked. Hayward wanted to be telling him there were no guarantees. Everybody was taking their chances.

"Tomorrow night we'll be sleeping like dogs in Fritz's dugouts," Hayward said, though without much force. "They're all right, from what I hear."

"In a month we'll be out of the front lines for good."

"What makes you think that?"

"I've got it figured out. You wait. See if I'm not right."

Hayward could hardly fathom how Myers was getting on. He was not convinced that he wouldn't suddenly topple back to the way he had been that morning.

"Perhaps so, Wilf." He stood up. "Perhaps we'll all be sent to some cushy spot with nothing to do but sleep and play bloody football."

He went for his cap.

"What you got to have is your faith in God,"

Myers said to him as he was about to go out the door.

"That's what keeps you going, is it?" Hayward fired his way.

"I had a long talk with the chaplain."

"What if you get a bullet in the head?" It was not like Hayward to be cruel, but he had to know how strong the man's armour was.

Myers wavered, but held on. "It won't happen."

"And if it does, you won't know a thing about it!"

Hayward left, disgusted with the fellow's damnable nerve in thinking he had it all worked out.

It was to his men he had to go. There wasn't the place for those questions when he was with the men. For what questions there were, they counted on him to have the answers.

The first person he saw was Bennett.

"I think you'll find everything in order, sir."

"Kits ready for storage?"

"Yes, sir."

"Let's take a look."

With the corporal at his side he began an inspection inside the barn. Each man's kitbag was packed and ready for delivery to the QM, and the barn had been shovelled and swept as clean as could be expected. Hayward thought it looked a good deal better than it did when they arrived. The men were quick to point out that a couple of the better carpenters among them had taken time to make repairs where the rain had been beating in.

Hayward could see more clearly the marks left on the walls and beams by his men, and the men of the other regiments who had rested there. In most cases it was initials, or the name of their regiment, or of their home town, but occasionally more elaborate evidence of their stay remained.

He pointed to a crude rendering of a caribou head. Cut with a pocket knife, it must have taken the man several hours.

"I didn't know, sir, until it was done. I know the men are not supposed …"

"Not to worry. It's rather good, don't you think?"

"Yes, sir."

"It's natural to want to leave something behind in a place that means something to you."

"I hadn't thought much about it, sir."

"In fifty, or seventy-five, or a hundred years, if the place is not rotted away by then, someone

will come along and know some Newfoundlanders have been here. Doesn't it sound right
for it to be that way?"

Bennett was taken aback by the directness
of the question and the earnestness in Hayward's
voice.

"I should say it does, Corporal. Right and
proper."

The men standing nearby, intrigued by the
talk between the two, exchanged sly, amused
glances. The corporal was beginning to look
uncomfortable, and Hayward brought them both
to other matters.

The first was Private Pendergast. Huddled
in a dark corner, the man appeared to be sound
asleep, and not the least bit aware of the figures
towering over him.

Bennett was about to use his foot to rouse
him, but Hayward held him back. "The poor
fellow needs a few hours to sleep it off if he's
going to be any use to us."

"He was making an awful racket last night.
I warned him, sir."

"I expect you did. They all learn after a while.
Isn't that right, Smith?"

The corporal hadn't noticed that Smith had

joined the crowd of men standing around, nor did he much like it that Hayward had singled him out from the others.

"He's just a young pup, what," said Smith. "He'll settle down after a spell."

"And what are you, then, Smith?" Bennett said sharply. "You were almost as bad, keeping all of us awake with your singing."

"The boys likes me singing, don't ya boys?"

Those around him responded with a robust endorsement.

"He sings the songs from home, sir, not jus' army songs. They're enough to make ya want to cry sometimes."

"I only wishes he had hes accordion, sir."

The corporal muttered something and shook his head.

Hayward caught his eye. "The private'll be singing a different tune soon enough, won't he, Mr. Bennett?"

Smith smiled. "I knows plenty of 'em, sir," he said. "I got 'em for all occasions."

Outside the barn, by themselves, Hayward declared that the corporal had done a first-rate job and told him it always happens that the men get restless before they go up the line. Hayward

knew Bennett would have to be crammed together with them in the stink of the trenches before
he'd really know what it was to be a corporal.

"Keep it in your mind, if something happens and I can't go on, you might be the one to
take charge."

"I know that, sir," he said, with a degree of
confidence Hayward didn't care for.

"And if you're hit, I want Smith in charge
of your section."

It set Bennett back a few notches.

"That clear?"

"Yes, sir."

Clarke came out of the house, carrying a
valise.

"It can't be that bad, old man," he said to
Bennett when he noticed the look on his face.

"No, sir."

"Would you see to it that this is brought to
the QM?" He handed him the valise. "Make sure
it's put with the proper lot. I wouldn't want
it lost."

"Yes, sir." The corporal took it and walked off.

Once he was out of hearing range, Clarke
declared, "They should make him a general and
have it over with."

"Lost our respect for the higher ranks, have we?" Hayward said.

"Tut-tut." Clarke smiled broadly. "We colonials are such an ungrateful breed."

Hayward had learned not to be surprised at anything Clarke said. "Tomorrow will tell the tale." He turned and walked into the house.

Clarke was right behind him. "Ah, but whose tale will it tell? That, chum, is the great question."

Hayward was in no mood to play at his game. "Why the hell did you join up, then, Clarke? Answer me that."

"Ah, a man who jumps straight to the heart of the matter. I admire that."

"You could have gone back to college."

"And miss out on it all? Father said I might regret it the rest of my life." He paused for a second, smiling to himself. "I suppose he meant if I didn't join, not if I did." He laughed.

Hayward began packing the last of his things into his valise. As much as he wanted to, he couldn't ignore Clarke standing there.

"We were a sorry lot the first few months," Hayward said, finally. "Didn't know what to make of us."

"Canadians, are ye?" Clarke mimicked. "Not bloody likely, sir."

"We came around."

"Tough lads, we were. All we needed was a few bull-headed limey brass willing to take us on."

"Scotland wasn't so bad."

"Scotland was bloody marvellous. Gallipoli was a proper pain in the ass."

"Remember how keen we were to go."

"We're still keen now, remember."

"Something's telling you it's going to be a bugger?" Hayward said.

"It always is. There's no guarantee of anything, is there?"

He wished Clarke had laughed at his apprehension, as he had expected he would. "Guaranteed shit. That's about all," Hayward said, in the way his friend might have said it.

Hayward flung his valise at the fellow. Clarke threw up his arms, but the bag struck him in the chest and fell with a thud to the floor.

"Bloody fool," Clarke declared with mock anger, booting the bag across the room. He looked at Hayward and sneered. "Let the Boche have at us, *n'est-ce pas?* What the hell do we care?"

Hayward was about to come back at him,

to jolt him still further out of his apathy, when he heard his name being called from downstairs.

"What is it?"

"The captain would like to see the both of you, sir. The new draft of men has arrived."

Hayward and Clarke looked at each other.

"Is something the matter, sir?"

"We're coming right down. Arrange to have my valise taken to the QM for storage. Straight away."

EIGHT

There were sixty-six of them, fresh that morning from Rouen. When Hayward and Clarke arrived, they were sitting about on their packs, having just been scrutinized by the colonel. They looked an eager lot, despite the tramp of the last few miles from the train station.

"Whelps," Clarke said under his breath. "Someone should have told them they had to be weaned before they could join up."

He led Hayward to a couple of the youngest-looking ones. "What part of Newfoundland are you from, men?"

"Trinity Bay, sir."

"Both of you?"

"Yes, sir. Him and me are cousins."

"And what brings you to this part of the world?"

"Pardon, sir?"

"Why are you here, then, Private?"

"The war, sir. We're here to do our bit."

"Ever hunt seals?"

"Lots of times, sir. I woulda had a berth on the *Stephano* this spring if I hadn't joined up."

"You know, this is a lot like sealing. Only the seals have guns, and they're just as smart as you are."

They looked at each other and laughed heartily.

Hayward knew their response would only sharpen Clarke's tongue even more. For the sake of the men, he diverted Clarke's attention to the sight of the colonel conferring with the commanding officers of the regiment's four companies. "They're splitting the pot."

They were about to join a group of other officers standing nearby when Hayward was approached from behind by one of the new men.

"Excuse me, sir."

He faced a private who looked to be no more than seventeen.

"Do you remember me, sir?"

He did look vaguely familiar, yet Hayward couldn't think where he had seen him before.

"Neddy, they all used to call me. Edward Martin. I lived up the street, in number 39."

"My God, Neddy Martin."

"Ned, sir, that's me name now."

"The fellow who almost broke his neck slidin' down the hill back of Kelly's Brook?"

"Yes, sir. The same one. I still got the scar." He pushed back his hair to show Hayward.

Hayward's mind was suddenly flooded with memories of growing up on Maxse Street. "He gave himself some smack," he said to Clarke. "We all thought he was dead. He came around just as we got him home."

"I was hoping I'd find you here, sir."

"But you're not old enough, are you?"

"Don't tell anyone, sir. A lot of us got away with it. I wasn't the only one."

"I bet you didn't want to miss out, did you, lad?" said Clarke with a slight smile.

"I made sure I wasn't going to be called a slacker. There's a good many of them a lot older than me, sir, marling around the streets in St. John's. It's people like you two, sir, that I want to be like. I think one day I might be an officer."

"That you will," Clarke said. "All it takes is persistence, and a good stretch of luck."

Hayward could see the captain looking their way, expecting them to assemble with the other officers from A Company. "We'll talk later, Ned. You'll have lots to tell me."

"You'll want to know about me sisters. They can't wait for you to get back."

"Sisters, is it," Clarke declared as they walked toward the others. "What's this about sisters?"

"He's got four."

"In that case we will certainly have to talk about Martin's sisters. They like men in uniform, do they?"

The captain was running down a list of names and matching them to sections of the four platoons. "A few of them you know from before. They're patched up and ready to go."

"I see Turner is back. He's got a bit of a limp. Not much, though, considering what they must have dug out of his leg."

"I should say he had a fine time in Wandsworth."

There was amused agreement all around.

"Who would say no to a Blighty one? Not I," said Clarke.

"What could be sweeter than a few months of English nurses?"

"If I may, gentlemen," the captain said, adding drily, "We do have other matters of equal importance on our minds."

"That we do, sir."

"The colonel has allocated us enough men to pretty well even up the numbers in each platoon. Turner can go back to his old section. The new lads I'm assigning as follows—"

"If it could be arranged, sir," Hayward interrupted, "there's a lad I wouldn't mind having with me. His name is Edward Martin. I believe you know his family, too, sir. Lived there at the end of Maxse Street. Johnny Martin's son."

The captain looked through his list as he spoke. "Short Johnny? The customs man with the four young daughters?"

"They've grown into fine young ladies, no doubt."

"And how would you know, Clarke?"

"Speculation, sir, having noted the glint in Mr. Hayward's eye."

Hayward started to blush, much to the delight of the others.

The captain continued to run his pencil

down his list. "And was there a glint in your eye, Hayward?" he asked matter-of-factly, but with a trace of amusement.

"Nothing compared to that in Mr. Clarke's."

All of them, including Clarke, broke into loud laughter.

"Good for you, Hayward."

"Something's gotten into the man."

The captain left to confer with the officer in charge of C Company and returned in the midst of Clarke's offer to act as go-between for anyone who might want an introduction to the Martin daughters when the war was over.

"You'll be happy to know, Hayward," said the captain, "that you can have young Martin. We did have to give up a tough-as-nails railway man to make the deal. However, we couldn't very well lose the opportunity for future and, shall we say, more attractive benefits. Isn't that right, gentlemen?"

"Indeed, sir," said Clarke. "Yet another thing to be fighting for."

The captain eyed him for the moment, but remained in high spirits. There was only the new draft of men to account for the captain's mood, as far as any of the officers could tell. Nevertheless, they took it as the sign of a promising afternoon, one in which they could relax, perhaps with a rousing football match and a little something afterwards to quench a good thirst.

It was left to the regimental sergeant-major to get the new men back in a decent formation and call them to attention so the colonel could have his final word.

The colonel stood before them, his gloved hands overlapped and resting against the silver knob of his ash-stick. He looked up and down the lines before he spoke. "Most of you, I know, have been anxiously awaiting this day. You could not have arrived at a better time. Before today is out you shall be part of the greatest show of the war and by this time tomorrow a part of our greatest victory. No soldier could ask for any more. I know I can count on you, just as I can count on every other man in our Newfoundland Regiment. When the going gets hard, think how proud of you every Newfoundlander will be, and how proud you should be of yourself, knowing what you're doing for God and your country."

The colonel's words, together with the distant echo of sporadic artillery fire, struck deep at the hearts of the new men. Even when he finished and had left it to the commanding officers of each

company to set out the details of the assign-
ments, the men stood rigid, awed, hanging on
to his words. It was indeed the day every one of
them had been thinking about since the moment
they volunteered. The words had been unlike any
ever directed at them before, coming as they did
from the very man who would lead them into
the enemy fire.

What finally broke the spell was the sergeant-
major spitting out their names and the platoons
to which they were now attached. As each man
fell out to collect his pack and report to the
officer in charge of him, Hayward saw the eagerness for battle that he only ever witnessed in
young men new to the Front. A few days before
he would have been thankful for such a display
of enthusiasm. Now he thought it showed in
their faces how very few of them had ever seen
gunfire or shrapnel tear at a man.

Young Martin drew up spryly in front of him
and saluted, his lips pressed together to prevent
his smile from widening any further.

"It's very good to have you with us, Martin."

"Thank you, sir. Everyone back home will
be very pleased when I tell 'em, sir. Especially
me mother."

He could recall Martin's mother. She had always been very pleasant to him. He remembered her as a tall woman, though perhaps she just seemed that way when she stood with her husband.

He and Clarke walked with Martin and the other men assigned to their platoons back to Madame Cornot's and the barns that would be their billets for the few hours they had before marching off again.

The old hands immediately made them feel welcome, and once it was found out from what part of Newfoundland they had come, in no time others showed up from that same part of the Island. If they didn't know them, they certainly knew of someone who did.

All the men wanted to hear what news they had of home. The new men were offered cigarettes, and someone directed them to a comfortable place in the shade, as everyone gathered around to hear what they had to say. It got so they could hardly keep up with the questions put to them, though there was no sign they minded being the centre of attention.

On this warm June day in France, it seemed odd to no one that their minds for the moment were with the spring seal hunt on the ice floes off the Newfoundland coast, or in the deep snows of the lumberwoods, slicing down black spruce with their bucksaws. For a St. John's lad like Martin the news was of what new sights there were to be had on Water Street, and what to make of the city's sporting rivalries now that so many of the keenest athletes had joined up.

NINE

Eventually Hayward got Martin together with Smith and Moss, in the hope that they would look out for him and see that he learned how things were done.

"You can muck in with us, bud," Smith told him, after Hayward had left. "Moss is not too keen on townies, seeing as he spent the first eighteen years of hes life in a dory, but that's no odds. We're all alike here."

"Don't be minding Smit'. Hes mouth is the biggest part of 'en."

Moss led him to the spot inside the barn that he and Smith had claimed for themselves. Martin laid down his pack. He dug his hand inside one of the pouches and came up with a can.

"Sardines. I bought 'em in Rouen. Figured

I'd save 'em till I got here. You fellows could do with a little something, could you?"

They immediately closed in, blocking him and his can of sardines from the eyes of anyone who might pass by.

"You're a fine fellow, bud. We could do with more like you."

"Look at that," Moss whispered as Martin opened the can and laid to view a double layer of the little fish saturated with juice and oil.

"The sight of a fin and you goes right off the head. Calm down." And with that, Smith poked his thick and callused forefinger into the can and came up with one of the slimy little creatures. He held it in the air for a second, then flicked it into his mouth.

"You arse." Moss needed no invitation either, and dug in for a taste of his own.

In a couple of minutes the can was empty, except for a bit of liquid, which they shared between them, draining it into their open mouths. They wiped away with the back of their hands the grease that had dribbled down their chins, and sat around then for a smoke.

Martin had with him some Woodbines, which the other two hadn't seen in weeks.

"You're a proper gentleman," Smith said, taking a deep draw and holding the cigarette in front of his face for an admiring stare.

"You fellows is all set to go?"

"You picked a fine time to show up, bud."

"I'm as ready as I'll ever be."

"None of us is ever ready," Moss said.

"What's it like, then?"

"You'll find out soon enough."

"Bad?"

"Depends."

"This time nobody knows. We're all the same —we takes what comes."

"The colonel must know."

Smith chuckled. "If he do, he's not lettin' on."

"Don't worry about it," Moss said in a tone wise and fatherly.

Martin persisted. "We're over first?"

Smith could see no point in having the fellow's questions continue. He noticed the corporal and called him over.

"Young Martin here needs to get it straight what exactly he's got to carry."

Bennett eyed Smith cautiously. "Is that so?"

"And perhaps you would be good enough to explain why we got such a load o' stuff. I don't have the brains to do it meself."

"Orders, Private." He took a piece of paper from a pocket. "Listen up, Martin. Rifle and your standard front-line gear, of course."

"He's fine up to that point, Corp."

The corporal glared at Smith, but continued. "Ammo—170 rounds, iron rations, two sandbags, two Mills bombs, tin hat, smoke helmet, water bottle, haversack, field dressing. You'll probably get a shovel, Martin, and a few flares. Maybe wire-cutters. And there's one sledgehammer left that someone has to carry."

"Lucky man."

Martin, not sure what anybody expected of him, quickly volunteered to take the sledgehammer. "And what might that be used for, sir?"

"That's in case you run out of ammunition," Smith said.

Moss laughed, and the corporal jumped on them. "You two figure it's a lark."

"You haven't got to worry about us!" Moss snapped, staring at him with contempt. "We'll do our part, and we'll do it as good as the next man."

Bennett turned to Martin. "Pack away everything else, everything. You're not to have any extra weight. And make sure you get one of those tin triangles sewn on your pack."

A look of disgust passed between the other two. The corporal did not see it. He had moved off, though not far enough for their liking.

"Tin triangles?"

"Orders, bud." Smith wouldn't tell him it was to make it easier for their aeroplanes to spot them if they got hit.

Having nothing better to do, Smith and Moss watched as Martin went through his belongings. He set aside anything that was to be taken with him. Occasionally he stopped and they discussed the merits of slipping in an extra something he might like to have if the going turned bad.

From one of the side pockets he removed an item that caused him to hesitate for a particularly long time. He tossed it over to Smith.

"Dr. Chase's Nerve Food." Smith started to chuckle. "Where in the name of God did you come up with that?"

"Me mom sent it. She said to use it only if I had to."

"You'll not be needing any Dr. Chase's Nerve Food."

"You're sure?"

Moss said, "Me grandfather took a douse o' that stuff before he had hes top teet' hauled out."

"Did it do him any good?"

"Not as I could tell. He was still as contrary afterwards as he was before."

Smith tossed it back to the young fellow. "Here, stow it away. Dr. Chase never had no whiz-bangs fallin' around hes ears when he made this stuff," he said, still laughing.

Martin smiled, though he couldn't enjoy the joke in the way the other two did. "At the base camp they used to talk about them," he said. "They told us you never knows they're coming till they're on top of you."

"It was a whiz-bang that got Critch. He never knew a thing."

It was the first time since he'd arrived that Martin heard the name of someone from the regiment who had been killed. He realized it shouldn't be bothering him, for there were a good many more who had met the same fate. When he looked at Smith and Moss he saw it was out of their minds as quickly as it had come in. Their interest was in what else he was about to uncover from his pack.

From the bottom he took out a small tin box

with the head of Queen Mary embossed on its lid. The other two were hoping to see sweet biscuits or peppermint candy inside, but were not surprised when he removed photographs from it. He passed one to each of them.

"You're a fine-looking lot, Ned."

"And that's Mother and Father," he said to Moss. "And Shep. She's a smart pup."

Moss was more interested in the picture of Ned and his four sisters that Smith was holding. "They're married, are they?" he said, snatching the picture away for a better look.

Martin shook his head. "Beatrice has a stuff-shirt who takes her to the new talking pictures at the Nickel. He wants to marry her. He knows he won't have a chance once the war is over."

"I'd try me luck with either one of 'em."

There was a coarse intake of air that Martin couldn't ignore. He pulled the picture from Moss's hand and quickly returned it to the tin box. "You shouldn't be talkin' like that about a fellow's sisters."

"No offence, chum."

"He don't mean nothing by it, bud," Smith said. "He haven't laid eyes on anything so pretty for a long time, that's all."

Martin packed into a kitbag everything he wouldn't be taking. When the others weren't looking, he slipped the pictures into the pocket of his tunic, then shoved the empty tin box into the bag and tied it up.

TEN

Hayward ran into them as they were leaving the quartermaster's, heading to the field for the football match. "I'll be there," he assured them.

"We might need you for goal, sir," Smith called to him.

Hayward liked football well enough, though he preferred sports in which he competed alone rather than as part of a team. In the Methodist Guards he had excelled at shooting and in 1912 he came close to winning the trophy given for the best overall score at the annual intercompany competition.

In the first week of the recruitment drive, before he joined the regiment, it was assumed by many that it would be only a matter of days before he signed up, given his skill with a rifle. When he did go to the Armoury and stood in line, he told everyone it had no influence on his decision, though looking back on it he knew that it must have.

For a while after he joined, when they started their training in Scotland, some of the others encouraged him to take a special course so that he might get to be a sniper. He wouldn't listen to them, and after a while it no longer was an issue. His shooting scores dropped off, and the officers who trained them ceased to believe that he was anything other than average.

He could not account for the decline in his marksmanship, other than to realize that it was all a lot different than shooting on a rifle range in St. John's, the other boys cheering him on when he struck the bull's-eye.

There had been times since then, however, when his skill with his Lee-Enfield had probably saved his life. He would never be sure, but he had seen the Turk fall just after several shots rang out, his among them. He had the definite feeling that his bullet was the one that had cut the man down. He had grown to accept it as fact. Every now and then he would think about the

Turk, and wonder if killing him meant anything other than what he had been trained to do. Only after the private who replaced him on sentry duty got it in the forehead did he stop thinking much about the Turk.

Hayward returned to the barn for a quick check on things before the football match. As he finished chatting to the few men still around, Bennett caught up with him. Hayward was determined that it would be brief.

"Is something the matter, sir?" Bennett said as Hayward was about to move off.

"What makes you ask that?"

"You don't seem to be yourself, sir."

Hayward smiled as if he was amused.

"You have a lot on your mind, I know, sir."

"Don't you?" Hayward said, hoping that would put him off.

"I can't say I'm looking forward to it, sir, but Fritz is in for a good fright."

It was not in Bennett to think otherwise, and Hayward knew it certainly wasn't his place to inject doubt where there was none to begin. He looked at him, not sure what to say, wondering whether he shouldn't just walk away and leave the man to his own conclusions.

In the end the corporal saved him the trouble. "If it's something private, sir, then I shouldn't be asking. I just thought maybe I could help, that was all."

"You're going to the match? I'm sure the men would appreciate the support. I'll be along."

Hayward left the barn and sat in the shade for a quiet smoke. He removed his cap and wiped the sweat from his face with a handkerchief. For a few minutes he saw no one, except for Pendergast, who had finally come to life and made the decision to brave the world outside. He walked across the farmyard, squinting and rubbing the back of his neck, oblivious of Hayward. He stopped halfway to have a stretch, then continued through the archway and onto the road.

When he was out of sight, Hayward yelled, "Have another one, Pendergast!"

From the upstairs window of the house it was Clarke who answered him. "You paying? In that case, order one up for me."

In a few seconds he came briskly out the door and joined Hayward in the shade. "I've been looking all over for you." In his hand he held two riding crops. "Are you game?"

"The captain would not be pleased."

"If he found out. Which he will not."

Clarke's one true source of delight in the army was the chance it gave him to indulge his passion for horses. Whenever an opportunity was presented to him, and at many times when it wasn't, Clarke was off on horseback, running errands for the colonel, or at least giving the impression he was. His greatest wish was to replace Lieutenant Steele as billet officer when he next went on leave and thereby be gone on horseback whole days at a time scouting out new billets in advance of the regiment.

Hayward was not easily convinced that they shouldn't be going to the football match instead.

"There'll be lots of time when we get back. Who knows, old chap, when we'll get the chance again?"

Hayward knew there was no way Clarke was about to change his mind. He would go on his own if Hayward didn't agree to go with him.

"What do you say? When you're up to your arse in mud in the bloody trenches you'll be wishing then you could be high and dry."

Hayward had to agree. And when he shook his head and grinned it was as good as saying yes.

They took a circuitous route to the stables,

one that avoided having to pass by the company's Orderly Room. They arrived to find Lieutenant Goodyear, a hulk of a fellow in charge of transport, cursing the higher ranks for not giving him enough men to do all that had to be done before the regiment moved off. He wore no tunic, only an undervest, rotten dirty and soaked in sweat.

"You got a half hour," he said to Clarke. "And get the hell back here on time. And don't wear 'em out or I'll have me mitts around yer bloody necks."

Clarke could only smile and remind him of the pint of whisky he had slipped him a few days before.

"A fine bit o' stuff," he said, just as gruffly. "Lucky for you it was, too."

"You're a good man."

He grinned, showing a set of teeth that looked like they could cut leather. "And you're a damn fool, Clarke, if you thinks you'll get off wit' being gone any longer."

They had the horses saddled and out of the stable with as much speed as looked good in front of the privates standing around, and before Goodyear got it in his head that there was some job he could use their help with.

They took a back road out of Louvencourt, then north through the countryside at a steady gallop, not stopping until they were well away from the village.

When they did stop and looked back at what they had left, it was with great relief, as if they had escaped something fearsome in pursuit of them.

Clarke, in high spirits now, waved one arm wildly above his head and galloped away again. He might well have ridden straight on for miles had not Hayward slowed down and pulled up under a small grove of trees.

Clarke slowed to a trot when he noticed Hayward missing, and circled back. "Be a sport, old man," he said jovially. "You don't have to always play by the rules."

At that he took off again, without another word to Hayward, who was left powerless to do anything but chase after him if he was not to be left alone.

Clarke rode hard, his body bent forward, through fallow fields, empty but for a scattering of magpies, with Hayward behind, yelling after him that he was a bloody lunatic.

When Clarke finally stopped, he did so

abruptly, on the edge of a stream, one that suddenly showed itself to Hayward, but one, he suspected, Clarke had known about all along. Its waters were swollen by the recent days of rain.

Hayward slowed down and trotted in behind him to a stop. They had clearly exhausted the horses. "There's somebody that's going to have your head yet."

But Clarke's mind was on nothing but the opportunity before them. "You're all for it?"

"What do you mean?"

"A dip, my man, a glorious dip."

Hayward surveyed the stream, then took out his watch.

By that time Clarke was off his horse and had him tied to the branch of a tree. He began to undress. "You are a Methodist prig after all, Hayward."

Hayward dismounted and tied his horse to the same tree. He stood watching Clarke struggle out of his boots.

"And what do you have to say for yourself?" Clarke asked, laughing.

"That's what you think, is it?"

Clarke removed his undervest and threw it at him. "You will have to come into that water and be saved yet again!"

And with that Clarke dropped his drawers and made a running plunge into the stream. His head burst the surface a few seconds later. He stood up, the water waist high. "It's bloody glorious! Come on, you fool!" He skimmed the surface with his hand, sending a spray of water far enough that the edge of it fell on Hayward.

Hayward didn't move an inch to avoid it, but then, as water dribbled down his face, he began to undress, with deliberate slowness, folding his clothes and setting them down on the grass.

He stood naked, the darkened skin on his hands and face a contrast to the milk-whiteness of the rest of him. His modesty allowed him only the time to suck in a lungful of air before he ran and jumped into the water. He blew the air out and let forth a teeth-clenching yell.

Clarke immediately splashed water into his face and chest, forcing him to turn away. His shoulders drew back stiffly, the water pounding his back, and then he fell forward into the water, his only escape.

He was up again as quickly as he had gone under, yelling at Clarke that he couldn't swim. Clarke only laughed at him. He disappeared under the water and, despite Hayward's efforts to get away from him, succeeded in yanking the fellow's feet off the bottom.

Hayward struggled to regain his balance, and broke the surface again, sputtering water and choking for air.

"You're a jackass, Clarke. And a damn inconsiderate one at that."

But he bore him no ill will, for to be naked in the running water was indeed a glorious thing. It soaked and soothed his skin too long soured by dirty clothes and in too many places scratched raw because of vermin bites. He slowly sank his whole body in it, letting the cool water envelop him, clearing his head for the first time since he woke that morning. He stayed under until his lungs could take no more.

Meanwhile, Clarke had swum upstream with a sharp and vigorous stroke. He let himself float back down. Hayward had to admire his abilities in the water, that and how he revelled shamelessly in the freedom of the moment. As he approached Hayward he uprighted himself, tremendously pleased still at coming up with such a place to swim.

"Our blood needed a good stirring up, old

man. What say we stay right here? Think they'd go ahead and have the war without us?"

"I have my doubts."

"Not that crowd, you're right."

They unleashed their laughter. They flung their arms about in a mock boxing match and in their revelry erased for the moment all thoughts of ever having to leave. When Clarke had no expectation of it, Hayward jumped at him and sent him flying, arms spread, backwards into the water.

When he surfaced, whipping his head free of water, anxious to avenge his pride, Hayward was sitting on the bank in the sun, well back from the water's edge.

Clarke cursed him and sent a spray of water in his direction as he walked slowly out of the stream. He sat down next to him and waited, like Hayward, for the sun to dry him off.

He wiped his hands in the grass and retrieved the cigarette case from his tunic pocket. They each lit one and sat surveying the countryside all around.

"In the trenches it's such a damn mess, you'd never think it could be the same place," Clarke said.

"It looks to be worth fighting for, wouldn't you say?"

"When you take the train across the Island you see places like this."

"Still, it's hardly the same."

"You're fightin' for that skirt of yours, are you, then?"

Hayward smiled. "I'm fighting. That's what I know. Neither one of us would be the one to let down the men, would we, now?"

Clarke seemed to accept that.

"And what do you think the Hun are thinking?" Hayward said. "The same as us?"

"They don't look any different than we do."

"I never had one to look at that wasn't dead."

"They take orders, they do their job, just like we do. So why are we killing the bastards?"

"So they won't kill us first," Hayward said. "Give them the chance and they would, every time."

"Well trained. Their generals must have done a good job on them."

There was a considerable silence before Hayward spoke again. "You've got it all figured out, then, Clarke?"

"Not me, chum. That's not what I'm here for."

Clarke turned over and let the sun pour down on the other side of him. "God, that sun is a wonderful thing, Allan."

For a long time they lay on their stomachs and gloried in it, putting off as long as possible the ride back to where they had to be.

ELEVEN

Lieutenant Goodyear dealt them a rough time, though no rougher than they expected. In any case, his attention was taken up with too many other matters to have it drag on for long. Clarke and Hayward slipped away and were on their way to the football match before he noticed they had disappeared.

The game was being played on the best of the several fields they'd been using since coming to Louvencourt. It was just off the main road, where it entered the village from Acheux. Beyond the field was the route they would be taking to get to the trenches, and, in the distance now, for those who cared to look, clouds of smoke could be seen. Most of the men watching the game chose to ignore it, as they did the occasional burst of artillery fire. Only once was the noise enough to divert attention from the game, and even then it was only for the moment it took to raise a cheer for whatever they imagined the field guns had done to the Hun.

The match was well into the second half when Clarke and Hayward showed up, having made a detour to dispose of the riding crops. Once they surmised the score—one to nought for A Company—they carried on as though they had been at the game all along, at the other end of the field.

Clarke quickly took a lead in stirring new life into the crowd, pitching insults at C Company's squad without mercy. "You got trench foot, the lot o' ya!" When that brought jeers from their supporters, he shouted all the louder. "Good kick! 'Tis a pity you didn't hit the ball!"

That fired up the officers from C Company, though they were no match for him. "You're a sorry state, Mr. Clarke. And your team is no better."

"Where did your crowd learn to pass like that? In a latrine, I'd say!"

When the laughter died away Clarke could see how much he had raised their ire, and he knew he had better be prepared to put up with the consequences, for they'd be sure to have back at him, one way or another. What saved him was the rush C Company made down the field, scoring a goal to tie the game.

At this point Hayward was called in to play goal, and much to Clarke's relief he made some admirable stops, enough that the game remained deadlocked at a goal each to the end. Had it been another day they might have stayed to break the tie, but it seemed now to all of them that a tie was fine as it was.

There were congratulations all around, with Clarke the most vocal of the lot, defusing the bite of his insults with offers to buy the other officers a slug of the best cognac they could get at the nearest drinking establishment.

Hayward, with the display he put on in goal, found himself surrounded by a cluster of his men.

"It was a fine job, sir," Bennett told him.

"Fine job, nothing," said Smith, knowing he could get away with it. "The man saved the game."

"I wouldn't go that far," Hayward said, though he was enjoying the attention.

"You come through for us when we needed you, sir."

"You can always count on Mr. Hayward, what. He knows what to do and he gets it done."

Hayward was left wondering how much of it was a tactic to keep the corporal in his place. Bennett moved off, as did some others, and when Hayward looked at the three left standing together, joking with him, he was struck by their need to have him as a friend and not just the man in charge of the platoon.

"You'll come with us now, sir, and have a drink?"

They knew he was intending to go with Clarke and the others, and in some ways it was a test of *his* need for them. There was no hesitancy in his reply.

"And which of you is going to pay for it?"

"I will, sir," Martin was quick to say. "Father said to me 'fore I left not to waste me money on bad habits, and I haven't much, either, but I knows he wouldn't mind me buying a drink for Allan Hayward, the church warden's son, now, would he."

Smith chuckled. "So that's why you don't go in much for the rum, sir."

"Mr. Hayward was as fine a Methodist Guard as there ever was. That's what Mother used to say."

"Your parents did a lot of talking, it seems," Hayward injected, laughing it off.

"It's nothing to be ashamed of, sir," said Moss soberly. "I considers myself a godly man. I lets out a scattered oath, but that's no odds."

Smith's face stiffened to keep himself from laughing out loud. He took the lead in getting them all to head off to the *estaminet*.

The *estaminet* was crowded and noisy. It had been the kitchen of a farmhouse, quickly converted into a public establishment with the addition of a few wooden tables and benches. Its grease-stained walls were covered with yellowed newspaper and wallpaper that had long ago lost its colour. A tiny window and the open door provided the only light.

Smith was well known to the old lady who ran the place, and when she saw him enter she quickly jostled together some of the men seated on the wooden benches, making enough space for the four of them at the long table that stretched down the centre of the room. Smith winked at her and gave her a cheery few words of broken French before she scurried to the stove where potatoes were frying.

The air reeked of grease and sweat and was

thick with cigarette smoke, but an *estaminet* was the closest most of the men had to a decent place to drink and it was the only place to find something other than army food to eat.

Martin was thinking they'd have some of the French beer, but the others had had their fill of it the night before. So with Smith as interpreter, he ordered up four glasses of *vin blanc* instead, a bit of grenadine in each to take off the edge.

"It's not bad," Martin said, after they had all taken a drink and he was waiting for someone to speak up.

"First-rate," Hayward told him, and Martin felt better.

The men next to them were eating fried eggs and chips, and farther along one fellow was digging into an omelette. That, together with bread, and sometimes soup, was the extent of the menu, unless one was lucky enough to have come in after the old lady had killed a chicken.

"Who'll have eggs and chips?" Hayward asked all of a sudden.

They looked at each other, not quite sure how he meant it.

"I'm saving mine," Moss said. "I figures I'm

going to need it more after 'tis all over than what I do now."

"Don't worry about it," Hayward said, and he ordered some for them all. "Make that another dozen of your mother's pork buns you owe me when we get back to the Island."

The mention of home did not touch off the chain of recollections Hayward expected it might. And it was muffled enthusiasm that greeted "Mayo" Lind as he came through the door. Lind was a bit of a celebrity on the Island for the letters he wrote about the regiment published in *The Daily News*, one of which had resulted in shipments to the regiment of free cases of the much-prized Mayo tobacco.

They made room for him at the table. "What lies are you writin' these days, Lind, ol' man?"

"Nothing that could make you fellows look good." He called for a cup of coffee.

"Put in a word or two about how much we miss saltfish and potatoes. Maybe someone will get it in their heads to send us some, what."

Everyone around the table was much amused, but it diverted only Martin from the eggs and chips. "Me mom and dad dearly loves your letters in the paper," he said, no longer able to contain his pride at being in Lind's company.

Lind, no doubt, had heard such sentiment before from men new to the regiment. It went by him without comment. He seemed preoccupied with the same things that lingered in all of their minds.

"It's never predictable. You know that, Lind, as well as any of us," Hayward said finally.

"As long as we keep in good cheer, that's the main thing," Lind said. "Right, lads?"

There didn't follow the robust endorsement that he had been expecting. Martin answered him, "I'll have me gunsight on a good many Fritzes, that's for sure. They can taste a few of me bullets for breakfast."

"That they will," Moss muttered, without looking up from his plate.

"There you go, Frank," Smith said. "You get down what the young fellow said. That's something they'll want to hear back home." He turned to Martin. "He'll be lookin' for you after 'tis all over to see how many you got. You'll have your name in *The Daily News*, bud, guaranteed."

Martin was enjoying the attention. He was picturing in vivid detail the reaction of his family to seeing his name in the newspaper.

"As long as you don't get your brains blowed out first, right, Martin?" Moss said. "The Casualty List—that's about the only way most of us'll ever get our names in the paper."

There was a chuckle from Smith, but when he saw the young fellow wasn't finding anything to laugh about, he cut it short. Martin glanced from person to person, looking to find someone who would look at him squarely. His eyes came around to Hayward a second time.

"Don't pay any mind to Moss. He'll never be on that list, especially if it's brains Fritz is aimin' for."

Martin took some relief in the fact that Moss was left with a crooked grin and without a word back at Hayward. The others made light of the march they had ahead of them, and Martin listened, eating what remained of his eggs and chips, though he had little appetite for it now.

"They've come up with another route," Lind informed them, between drinks of his coffee. "Fritz's artillery's been pounding the one we were s'posed to take. The colonel sent off someone this afternoon to scout out a new one, off the main road. We're keeping clear of Mailly-Maillet from what I hear."

It was news to them all, although only Hayward was surprised at not having heard it before. Lind was obviously in good with a lot of higher-ups.

"We should at least *get* there in one piece," Moss said, "even if we don't stay that way." He banged the table with his fist and let out a guffaw. He said to Martin, with complete seriousness, "You got to laugh at it. You won't get through it if you don't."

There was nothing Martin would say for fear of sounding timid and without spirit, and, worse still, cowardly.

He knew he was no coward, and he wasn't about to let anyone get away with thinking he was. Ever since he joined up he'd been a keener. They all said so in training.

"Don't be worrying about me," he told Moss. "I'll have me laugh out of it yet."

The old lady who ran the place came over to see if there was something more she could get them. Her smile further creased her face, cheering them, as a grandmother's might. Smith, favourite that he was, reached out to take her hand. Embarrassed, she wiped her hand front and back across her apron before letting him hold it. He patted it gently, and spoke with a brash show of affection, in a voice loud enough for everyone in the room to hear.

"Our dear *Madame,* you are *très bon, très bon.* Your heart is *comme le soleil* ... in the sky. Your *estaminet* is *très bon,* the best in all of Louvencourt."

As amused as they all were by Smith's bad French mixed with his broad Newfoundland accent, it occurred to nobody to laugh, for their fondness for the old lady was genuine.

"Merci, Madame, merci."

Smith broke into a song he had sung in the *estaminet* many times. It was one he knew she loved, though of course, she did not understand the words.

"There was hard tack, cognac, heavy
      packs, and no slack,
Bread and omelettes, sour beer and tea!
Trench feet, bully beef, potatoes fried in
      bacon grease,
'Baccy smoke and nar bit o' meat at the
      Louvencourt Soirée!"

Smith was on his feet with a sprightly step

dance, which ended in the loud stomp of one foot against the wooden floor. A boisterous cheer rang out and the whole crowd broke into another song for which Smith had composed new words.

> "Our dear Madame from Louvencourt,
>   parley-vous!
> Our dear Madame from Louvencourt,
>   parley-vous!
> Our dear Madame from Louvencourt,
> She'll be cookin' it for forty years more,
>   inky-pinky, parley-vous!"

By the end of it the old lady had her apron to her face and was wiping away the tears. "Naughty boysss!" she said. She planted a kiss on Smith's cheek, then took a playful swipe at him when he offered his lips. She scurried back to the stove, which by now had a cloud of smoke rising from it.

As he left the *estaminet* with the others, Smith waved goodbye and sang out to her, "And she'll be burnin' it for forty years more, inky-pinky, parley-vous!"

Martin thought it great sport. On the way back to the billet he made a point of walking with Smith. Smith held out a cigarette to him.

"I try not to smoke much. Me mother ..."

"Yer mother is right. Me missus is always on about it to our fellow."

"What fellow?"

"He's fifteen. Fine young lad he is, too."

It took Martin a while to think of Smith as a father, especially to someone only two years younger than himself.

"Is he going to join up?"

"He took me place as shareman till I gets back. Doin' all right wit' it, too. There's a few fish. Someone's got to look out to the family."

"You wouldn't want him at it?"

"You'll do fine, bud. Stick wit' me and Moss and there won't be nothin' you can't deal wit'."

"It's just that it's me first time and all."

"Don't be thinkin' about it. You goes through it once and you're laughin'."

He felt better talking to Smith. Smith seemed to know how much he was missing the buddies he'd made in training. A couple of them had been with him at the base camp in Rouen, and one was even part of the new draft like himself, but he was assigned to another company and Martin hadn't seen him since they were split up. His best chum was still in England some-where, held back like a lot of others, for what reason nobody seemed to know.

"I'll have that smoke now."

Smith took it as a good sign and he prompt-ly yelled ahead to Moss to hold off walking like it was a feed of saltbeef and cabbage he was going to instead of whatever the hell the army had scrounged up for their last meal.

"Eat while you got the chance," Smith said to the young fellow. "That's rule number one."

"If it don't move on your plate, eat it," said Moss. "If it do, stab it, and eat it anyway."

"You'll have the poor fellow drove off his head," Hayward told them, though Martin was smiling now.

"All the more for us, eh, Smithy?"

When Hayward left them, on his way to the Orderly Room, Martin looked more a part of it all than he had at any time since he'd come. A lot of it was Smith's doing, Martin realized that. But no odds; he took another draw of the ciga-rette and wondered aloud what was for supper.

TWELVE

The Orderly Room was crowded. The officers were standing about in groups of twos and threes, their conversation subdued. It was broken frequently by mild laughter, and by the raw coughs of men who could have done with a few more days of dry weather.

Hayward joined Clarke and another officer who had only recently entered their ranks as a second lieutenant. The fellow was in the midst of relating something about battalions of German reinforcements heading toward the front lines.

"It's only a rumour, of course."

"Aren't they all?"

"You wouldn't want it to be too easy, now, would you, Clarke?" Hayward said. "There has to be some opportunity for you to display the pluck you learned in that school of yours in England."

"Ah, Hayward, at last you've uncovered a sense of humour. That female company you keep must be making a new man of you."

Hayward's smile broadened. He'd let it rest. He knew Clarke would drag it on endlessly if he didn't.

The captain had taken up a position near the centre of the room, where he could be seen by everyone. He had taken some time to shave again and have his hair trimmed. He was looking particularly well groomed and confident.

"I'm sure you must all feel relieved. I do. It's time to get on with it, get done what has to be done. A few of you, I know, have doubts about just how easy it's going to be. I'm not one of them. We have our orders. I know what our men are capable of. I know we're all going to give a good account of ourselves. And for damn well sure the Hun have gotten the wind blown out of them by now, after what our artillery has been sending over all week."

Most of the officers were surprised at the captain. He was known to take particular pride in the fact that he hardly ever swore in front of his men, no matter how mildly, and never in the way that was common to most of them.

"Everything is set to go. We have our job to do and we'll do it and do it well. A Company will have a lot to be proud of when the day is over. I have no doubt about that whatsoever. And nor do any of you."

They weren't sure he had come to the end of it. But when the silence went on for longer than seemed necessary, someone finally shouted, "Well done, sir!" The rest followed with a cheer.

"There's not one of us who'll be anywhere but in the thick of it, alongside you, sir."

"That we will, chaps. You can be sure of that," another chimed in.

The captain was looking pleased to have stirred them up a bit.

Clarke had not raised a cheer as loud as the others, Hayward noticed. The captain and he had done little more than tolerate each other since the captain had taken charge of the company, although it had not yet reached the point of hard words between them.

Hayward was all set to take a swipe at Clarke for his lack of goodwill when through the door came the colonel. His arrival was unexpected, even for the captain, as was obvious by the irregularity in the captain's step when he walked over to greet him.

"Gentlemen," he said, removing his hat. The captain offered to take it, but the colonel held him off for the moment, preferring to hold it under his arm until he had removed his leather gloves. He placed the gloves inside the hat and handed it to the captain with a slight nod of his head. "You're all keen for a run at the Kaiser's boys, I suspect."

There were a few hesitant chuckles until the colonel smiled, and they realized it was an attempt at being light-hearted. The laughter rose to something more substantial.

"The Kaiser's boys are in for a bad surprise, sir," someone called out, and that brought noisy approval all around.

The colonel's smile set firmly into his face. He was being more congenial than any of them had been used to. It came as a considerable relief to many in the room, who had expected his sudden arrival to mean a report of new problems with the advance to the Front.

"I spoke to the major-general less than an

hour ago and he asked me to pass on to you his regards," the colonel said, his tone more spirited than any of them had ever heard it. "He wishes you to know that Headquarters is supremely confident that a great victory is at hand. And on your behalf I assured him that we stand ready and more than able to do our part in bringing that about."

There was a round of applause led by the captain, which seemed to please the colonel, though it failed to broaden his smile any.

"Some of you are what you would call old hands at this game. For others this will be the first time leading your men to the Front. Let me say, as someone who's done it many times, nothing can make you prouder as an officer than to be charging off across the field of battle, side by side with your men, all of you out there giving everything you have for your regiment. It is the best feeling an officer will ever know."

This generated a show of enthusiasm, though it tended to be the newer officers who displayed most of it.

"I want you to do your very best. That is all I can ask. I will do the same for you."

When Hayward glanced at Clarke he could

tell that he was not among those who seemed eager for more such encouragement from the colonel. He could never have anticipated, however, what took place next.

"Sir," Clarke said, raising his hand slightly to indicate who was speaking. The captain gave him a hard look, but Clarke did not flinch.

"The colonel must only have a few moments to spare with us," the captain said, his displeasure but partially disguised.

"I do have the other three companies to attend to. Well, what is it, Clarke?"

"Is it true, sir, that there are very few gaps in their wire?"

This question had been on the minds of all the officers, and, though they'd dared not show it, they were admiring of Clarke's nerve in raising the matter directly to the colonel.

"And just what gives you that idea, Clarke?"

"The reports from the raids, sir. And there have been new rumours ..."

"The raids took place three days ago, did they not? And as for rumours—the army doesn't operate on rumours, Mr. Clarke. It has the artillery to take care of rumours. And furthermore, let me remind you that you have a platoon of men under your command, and not for one second do I want to think that there would be any hesitancy on the part of your men because they had wind of somebody's rumours. I hope that's clear."

Clarke chose not to say anything. But the colonel stared at him and Clarke could see he was expecting some show of humility.

"Very clear, sir," Clarke said. Only Hayward was close enough to hear him groan under his breath.

"And who else of you has a question?" the colonel said stiffly.

There was only a dutiful silence, which the colonel broke with a brusque few words to the captain to indicate that he would now have his hat and gloves.

"I shall see you all at 9 o'clock. Prepare yourselves for a damn fine routing of the Hun."

He left as abruptly as he had entered. The stir of conversation gradually returned to the room, yet no one cared to comment when Clarke declared, seriously it seemed, "I'm always ready for a damn fine rout."

Clarke had his back to the captain, though he must have known the captain could only be further galled by anything he said.

It was Hayward, with uncharacteristic forcefulness, who saved Clarke from being set upon. "Admit it, Clarke—you won't be satisfied unless you come out of this with a medal hanging from your breast pocket. You're in it for the glory. And it's glory you shall have."

Clarke made a start to defend himself, but was drowned out by the shouts of support that Hayward's taunting received from the other officers. It was their chance to break the tension brought on by the colonel's visit. Eventually, Clarke shrugged it off, with good-natured indifference. He had nothing further to say.

It was only later, away from the Orderly Room, when he and Hayward were on their way to the mess for the last meal before the regiment moved off, that Clarke's spite was let loose.

"Bloody charmer. He'd have us string ourselves up on that wire, I suppose!"

"The artillery will have done the job on the wire by now."

"You think so!"

"The colonel's not the one making the decisions."

"He damn well has to carry them out."

"I'd say he doesn't like it any better than you do."

"It'd take a bloody mind-reader to figure that out. The man's not willing to lay out the whole story."

"Maybe he doesn't know it all. He could be in the dark as much as we are."

"Whatever the hell he does know he's keeping to himself. We're only the ones who've got to rout the Hun, remember. We don't need to know, because we haven't got the brains to handle it if we did."

His venom was too strong not to have it play around Hayward's mind after the fellow had finally stopped and they were walking on without a word between them.

"And what difference does it all make?" Hayward said after some distance.

"Not a damn bit. That's it, don't you see! We're in it now, and we do what we have to do." He was almost laughing. "We have a meal, we wash up, we go to war."

"Very simple."

"Even an officer from the colonies can understand that."

THIRTEEN

The meal was, by normal standards, a splendid affair. The officers had pooled their money and instructed the cook to treat them to something special. They had no idea how he came up with it all. The man had his ways and they knew better than to ask about them.

He had taken extra care with setting out the table as well, even to the last-minute addition of a few wildflowers in an earthen jar. It took on the air of a banquet, and as the officers wandered in, in twos and threes, a certain formality settled about the room.

While they awaited the arrival of the captain they contented themselves with sampling a bottle of the prime champagne acquired from the officers' canteen.

"Pity we can't make a night of it."

"Now, then, let's not sour things."

Indeed, before long, they were all determined to make the evening something to be remembered. The conversation grew spirited, charged with stories of the company's exploits since the war began. They lingered over the humorous ones, recalling with particular relish an episode in Cairo when one of them had to be wrested from some drunken sergeant of the Australian Light Horse. The fellow was hellbent on making him pay for suggesting that a one-armed Newfoundlander could bareknuckle it with an Aussie any time and come out the winner.

The captain, as he came through the door, heard only the last few words. The story's conclusion—in which the Aussie was labelled "a dirty swaggering sleveen" and left with a bloody nose skewed to one side—had been so often repeated that the captain instantly added, "You can be sure they didn't have to ask the whereabouts of Newfoundland again."

"The Aussies and us—the best of friends after that."

Someone handed the captain a glass. He

raised it awkwardly. "So, here's to you, men."
He drank it down in one go, then used the edge
of his forefinger to wipe what had trickled onto
his moustache.

"Steady as we go then, lads."

"Yes, and that we will."

The meal started with the captain bestowing
a firm and solemn blessing, then a long pause
awaiting his "amen". A chorus of amens followed, and the scrape of chairs as all the com-
missioned officers of A Company seated themselves.

They faced an array of platters—roast chick-
en with dumplings in the centre of the table,
flanked by mounds of vegetables—and bowls
of steaming gravy. There were bottles of good
red wine and plenty of bread, of course, and
coffee. They dug into it with great gusto.

"Outdid himself, he did."

"An extra's day's leave, is it, sir?"

But the greatest treat came at the end of the
meal, the raisin pudding—the figgy duff.

"And hot molasses sauce to top it off."

"She's a corker. Leave it to the man here to
buck us up with the good old grub from home."

"Better than mother herself could make."

The cook was happy enough to be able to do that much for them, and think nothing of it. They dug into it like ravens and went on endlessly about it after the last lick was gone. They could only think how right it was that when they headed off it would be with memories of a home-cooked meal.

"Ah, this is it," said Clarke, his chair pushed back from the table, sipping cognac and lighting up a panatella. "The incessant joys of army life. Would we have it any other way? Not I. Hot soaking baths be damned. A pint of English lager? A paddle boat on the lake, a coquettish young thing eyeing you from the stern … who needs it?"

"Clarke, we'll not have you spoil it all. The other we can do without. But take back the bit about the girl."

"Yes, old man, that's overdoing it. Not the girl. On a hot summer day, was it?"

"With the rain coming on. Then having to go to shore for shelter."

"In the woods."

"I'll take back the girl, then."

Around the table there wasn't a man who didn't light up the best he had, and linger on each taste of cognac. Only Myers seemed unwilling to join in the idleness. He removed himself inconspicuously to a corner.

"I have it on good source that we're on to something cushy after this."

"I wouldn't bet on it."

"I don't know about you crowd, but there's a week in Edinburgh for me."

"She has you forgotten by now, old man. It's been ten months."

"She's taken up with some other bloke in training, I'd say. What about it, boys? He won't get a look in."

"Not a prayer."

"That's not what the letters say."

"Ah, the famous letters. The letters that nobody's laid eyes on."

"They won't, either."

"Read us one."

"Not likely."

"We could do with a chuckle."

"I'll be the one laughin'. All the way down Princes Street."

The captain had chosen to give way to the few that were in a talkative mood, though he seemed to have no mind for what they were on about. This didn't escape Clarke, who, Hayward could see, was feeling more and more the urge to stir things up.

"I'll tell you something," said Clarke when they had exhausted the discussion of how much of any love letter to believe.

"And what wonderful bit of wisdom does the man have for us this time?"

Hayward tried to head him off with a sharp look across the table, but Clarke only winked at him.

"I think we're damn lucky. The Newfoundland, right in the midst of it. Johnny-on-the-spot, sir."

Hayward, and the others, waited for more. The captain stiffened.

Clarke calmly raised his glass in a toast. "Here's to you all. There when it counts. Determined to do ourselves proud."

"And what about you, Clarke?"

"Headlong into it, by God. Gone like a bullet at the whistle."

The glasses rose around the table in a grand manner. Myers came out of the corner and joined in, though he had nothing in his hand and seemed lost in the robust cheers that followed.

The meal ended with them all draining their

glasses. The captain stood up and retrieved his cap. The others rose and put their minds to leaving. At the door the captain, setting his cap firmly on his head, bid them a good evening.

"I shall see you at 9 o'clock. It'll be a fine time, gentlemen."

He left, and the others were not long behind him. Only Myers lingered, wanting Hayward to do the same. Hayward told him squarely that he had no time, and was out the door and catching up with Clarke before Myers was on to him again.

FOURTEEN

Williams and the others manning A Company's cookers had come up with a bit of a treat for the regular men as well. "It being yer last an' all," he said to Smith.

"Last what, chum?"

"Last together like this for a while, he means," said Moss.

"Just checkin'." Smith grinned. He forked through the stew and came up with something. "And whata we got here? Real meat! I don't believe it. Hindquarter o' rat. Looka that now, will ya."

"We went through a lot o' trouble, Smithy," Williams growled as he slopped a pile of the stew into the next man's mess tin.

"And, please God, you will again." Smith took some bread and found a place in the evening sunlight to sit down.

"I can't eat," said Martin, who had taken a spot next to him.

"You got to, bud. You never knows when you'll have the chance again."

"I got no stomach for it."

Moss was sitting nearby. "It was like that wit' me the first time goin' up the line," he said through a mouthful of the stew. "An' what I did eat I couldn't keep down."

"Job's comforter," Smith said.

"You got to give it a try, all the same. It'll do you some good whether you likes it or no."

"It mightn't sound like it, bud, but Mossie's talkin' sense. It's gonna be a long march. You'll be wishin' you had somethin' in your gut when we gets on the move."

Martin had a half-hearted go at what was in his mess tin. But when the other two had finished, he was still left with a large portion of it uneaten.

"Give it here, then," said Moss. "No use wastin' it." He took Martin's mess tin and polished off the stew.

"Cast-iron gut," Smith muttered.

"Williams," Moss called out, "what else you got?"

"Pork toutens wit' yer tea, lads. Fried in bacon grease."

At the mention of the toutens—buns made with bits of fatback pork—Williams was descended upon from all sides. That they were still warm, some of them, and were offered with a coating of molasses caused an even greater stir.

"By God, you'd think they had their fortune." Smith was there to get one nevertheless, and encouraging Martin to do the same.

"Now, you can't pass up on a touten," Moss said to him, with a clear indication that if Martin couldn't finish it, he certainly would.

"This is to shut us up bellyaching about the food for a few hours, that's all this is." Smith licked his fingers of the molasses. "Good, though."

Martin swallowed the remaining bit of his, to Moss's disappointment. The three of them sat in the sunlight, drinking tea and smoking Martin's cigarettes. Their figures cast long, indistinct shadows.

"What a day, what a day."

"What an evening to catch a few trout."

"Not a draught o' wind, not a draught."

"I'd say we're in for another fine one tomorrow. Look at that sky."

They took in the lull and the wonderful reddish sky a while longer.

"And how's it going?"

It was Hayward. They had trouble seeing him standing there in the glare of the sun.

"Finest kind, sir."

"Grand evening, idn't it, sir?"

"That it is."

"We could use a few more o' these."

"That we could." Hayward looked at Martin, who hadn't yet said a word.

"Hes stomach is not right," Smith put in. "Nothin' to worry about. He'll work it off."

"Nothin' atall to it, is it, Ned?" Moss said, slapping a hand on his back.

If the truth were told, Martin was thinking, they were none too calm themselves. They were better at talking their way out of it, that was all it amounted to. "You haven't got to be worrying about me," he said to Hayward.

"That's the ticket, Ned," said Moss. "He'll be number one."

"And I can talk for meself!"

He considered it no measure of his back-
bone that he wasn't like Moss, stuffing himself
like a half-starved dog. Or Smith, for that matter, who seemed never to find a reason to get
bothered about anything. He'd be able to work
it out in his own good time.

Hayward motioned him aside. If there was
something to be said to him, he'd just as soon it
be said in front of the others. He didn't take to
being singled out. Nevertheless, he went with
the officer, off along a footpath that wasn't much
used, where no one would overhear whatever it
was Hayward had on his mind.

"And so what about it, Ned? Think your
sisters will take to their young brother in a
uniform?"

"Didn't think too much of me joinin' up.
Mother neither."

"Get back home and it'll be a different story.
You won't stop them fussing over you."

"And you, sir. Wait till they find out it's you
that's in charge. I tried to write this afternoon,
but I couldn't. I will in a couple of days."

"I'd say the two of us, strolling down Maxse
Street, will turn a few heads."

"For certain."

"It'll be all we can do to keep up with the offers."

"The offers?"

"To come for dinner, and the parties."

"I don't expect so, sir, not me." Almost before he finished, he had changed his mind. "I suppose so, sir."

He was having trouble getting his mind to settle on it. What Hayward had stirred up began to fade.

Hayward was hard pressed to get him to speak about much else, other than the trek to the trenches, and how he was sure it wouldn't bother him any to carry such a load.

"I'm used to it," Martin said. "It's no trouble."

"You'll do fine."

"It's not the load. You know, I wouldn't want Father to think I wasn't doin' me part, the same as the next fellow."

"Your father knows the difference of that."

"I expect so. It's the way I get, you know."

Hayward told him about his own first time in the trenches, in Gallipoli, how none in the regiment knew what to expect. "We all had it bad. But after a while we got over it, just like you will, give you a couple of days."

"I've been thinkin' that."

"A far cry from home, this place is. But you'll not be sorry you came. Think what stories you'll have."

Hayward caught himself about to say that one day Martin would look on it all as a great adventure. He gripped the private's shoulder momentarily and passed him an encouraging look, magnifying it with a broad smile.

It did something to calm him down. He looked straight at Hayward, and seemed to find relief in his good spirits.

"That's the stuff, chum."

But the private's thin smile was gone in seconds. "I'm thinking there'll be a good many like me."

"Lots worse."

Hayward could only hope he would work it out during the tramp up the line.

"I can see us back home again. Both of us. I can picture that, sir," Martin said quietly as they came in sight of the others.

FIFTEEN

There was not much time before the march-off, and Hayward for certain would have to see Marie-Louise.

He sent Lucien to find her. In just a few minutes the boy returned, out of breath, waving his arms, drawing too much attention to himself. Hayward quickly led him aside, gripped the boy's arms and forced them to be still.

"Settle down, laddio."

"*Allez à la maison,*" Lucien sputtered. "*Sa mère, elle n'est pas là.*"

Hayward shook his head.

Lucien repeated it more slowly while he struggled to get free. Finally he stood perfectly still, narrowed his eyes and grinned in an unmistakable imitation of Marie-Louise's mother. "Gone, no mudder. You go. *Allez. Allez. Vite!*"

Hayward released him, but not before heading him in the other direction. The boy walked away, laughing to himself.

Hayward gave a quick whistle. "No more stories, laddio. Secret."

"Secret, *oui*, big secret." Lucien winked at him. "No more bread, laddio."

Hayward eyed him stone-faced, Lucien grinning all the while. Hayward shook a fist at him, though he should have known better, for Lucien liked nothing more than a playful boxing match. The boy came after him full-force.

Hayward dodged his flying fists, then grabbed him, tickled him mercilessly, and sent him off once again.

The walk to Marie-Louise's house was awkward business. Twice he was forced to stop and engage in trifling bits of conversation with other officers. Each time his quick departure brought on a string of coarse remarks about just where he might be headed. He scoffed at some, and walked on, pretending not to hear the rest.

To slip into the enclosure unnoticed required careful timing, and only after stopping nearby on the pretence of having to adjust part of his uniform did he manage it. He proceeded cautiously, unsure whether Lucien's message could be trusted. There was no sign of anyone. He wandered into the barn and came face to face with the milk cow. The beast blared at him.

As he retreated his eyes fell on Marie-Louise standing shyly in the doorway to the house. She was without a bonnet or apron, and dressed in a white blouse, the collar and cuffs edged with lace, and a long black skirt, as the young women of the village would wear on Sundays. She looked at him for a moment before slipping inside. He thought it an apparition.

He rushed to the doorway, without knowing what to expect. It was her, now sitting on a bench near the kitchen window, in the pale yellow light coming through the curtain.

He sat beside her on the bench. She bent her head, staring at her hands, continuing to do so even when he took hold of one of them.

Lifting her hand, he pressed it against his dry lips. She looked up, and was about to speak, but he touched his forefinger to her mouth.

He embraced her, placidly at first, then with more strength, without any thought to whether someone might discover them. He shut his eyes, and kissed her passionately on the mouth. She clung to him, her hands clenched about his neck.

When they heard the far-off sound of artillery she hummed in his ear. His heart pounded faster. He kissed her and held her head against his chest.

SIXTEEN

Hayward saw her again along the roadside when the regiment marched out of Louvencourt. She was standing motionless behind her mother, who waved a handkerchief and shouted encouragement to the men tramping by. She seemed unsure it was him, but then he remembered he wasn't in officer's uniform. He called her name and she threw her hand in the air.

Hayward didn't care that he fell out of step. He knew he couldn't go past without one more memory of her. Their eyes fixed on each other as he walked back. There appeared on her face a quivering, reluctant smile.

"Au revoir," he called cheerily, and ran to catch up with his men. He side-stepped his way

back into formation.

Not long before, with 9 o'clock drawing nearer, the regiment had assembled for the march-off, all but the ten percent of men held back on orders from Headquarters. In small groups, with the sun about to touch the horizon, they drifted together from the billets throughout the village. They said little, mostly words of regret at leaving Louvencourt once again.

The officers had changed into uniforms of the regular soldier so the German guns wouldn't be able to single them out. In the farmyard Hayward and Clarke said their farewells to Madame Cornot. She embraced them both and told them she would pray every night for God to keep them safe.

They shook the hand of the old man. *"C'est la guerre. C'est la guerre,"* he said. He squinted and bent his already crooked forefinger in the air several times as if firing a rifle.

They tousled the hair of young Lucien. The boy's lip trembled. Hayward took him aside and told him he was sure to see him before long, repeating it until he was certain the boy understood. Into his hand he tucked a coin, a Newfoundland twenty-cent piece with King

George V on it, one Hayward had kept since leaving home. Lucien looked it over with great curiosity.

"For good luck," Hayward said to him. *"Bonne chance."*

"Bonne chance, laddio," the boy said. He wouldn't look at Hayward again, and ran off behind the barns.

Hayward and Clarke took to the road. They lit cigarettes and walked in silence to where the regiment had been gathering. By the time they arrived most of their men had congregated near the head of the line, in anticipation of the order for A Company to fall in.

Martin stood by himself, looking around him at the hundreds of men along both sides of the road. He took in the rise and fall of their voices, the storytelling, the laughter, the advice given and passed along. He watched as some checked their equipment, and others sat alone on the grass, smoking.

When the bugle sounded, Martin was one of the first taking up his position.

"No flies on you," said Smith as he and Moss joined the line. "You likes a good tramp after dark, Ned?"

"Don't bother me none."

"It do me, then," said Moss, trying to balance the weight of his pack, cursing until he
got it right.

"This is it now. This is the big one." Smith
said it with a certain ceremony, as if it were
possible to heighten the emotion any further.

The others fell in, four abreast, and the roll
call began. Up and down the line, there resound-
ed the quick fire of the platoon sergeants and
the answers snapping back.

In the distance could be heard the approach
of another regiment. The roll call continued
without a second's pause, until the tramp came
so near it could no longer be ignored. The regiment marched past, a good many hands raised
in the air. It was a regiment they had shared
trench-digging duties with not many days before.

"We'll save a spot for ya, lads," called one.

"Yes, b'ys, keep 'er clear for the Newfoundlanders."

"We shan't start without ya."

"We'll have a yarn in Fritz's dugouts."

The roll call resumed as the tramp of boots
faded. With the end of it, word was passed along
that all had been accounted for—close to eight

hundred men. The officers took their posts. The ten percent held back looked on from the sidelines, sorely disappointed not to be part of it.

The colonel's steed was brought forth. He mounted it and rode with slow and deliberate precision to the head of the line. There were no words spoken, only a look of unflinching confidence, a stiff declaration of what he was expecting. He waited until it had permeated the entire regiment. He turned and, with a wave of the gloved hand gripping his stick, started the march through Louvencourt.

Martin was feeling again what he had felt on his arrival that afternoon. His trust was eagerly given. All his months of training had been directed to this, and he had known long ago that when the time came he would be up to it.

He showed a strong and lively step during the two minutes they marched at attention through the village. He did not avert his eyes to the townspeople as the others were doing, for he had not made the acquaintance of any of them. It was just as well, he thought. It reminded him of the farewell given him and the others when he left home.

He was surprised to see Lieutenant Hayward quit the line for a few seconds to call to some girl standing along the way. When he returned, Martin saw it took the man several steps to regain his stride.

On word from the colonel, an order rang out that they could march at ease. With rifles slung, the intensity of the moment passed, and on they went. As the last of the troops marched past the church and out of the village, in the fading twilight, the whole regiment broke out in song. In voices as strong as ever they raised they sang the strains of an old favourite, "Keep the Home Fires Burning."

Smith called it "some wonderful sight" and said, as the song was almost at an end, he was sure he'd never see or hear anything so good again. Martin had been caught by the vigour of the singing and wanted just to march along in the rhythm that lingered.

Neither did Moss have much to say, leaving Smith to content himself whistling the tune with some others, who, like them all, were hoping to keep their minds off the weight of their packs.

Eventually he started up another song. It took hold, though not with the same fervour, for their section of A Company was rather close to the colonel.

"I'm Hadow, some lad-o,
Just off the Staff,
I command the Newfoundlanders
And they know it—not half!
I'll make them or break them,
I'll make the blighters sweat,
For I'm Hadow, some lad-o,
I'll be a general yet!"

Martin hadn't heard it before, and it was only on the second go-round that he got all the words. He gave it a try, Smith urging him on, the two of them belting out the last line with a vigour that turned the colonel's head.

From atop his horse the colonel caught Martin's eye. It startled the private for the second, until he saw a fleeting edge of a smile beneath the moustache. When the colonel turned back he said a few words to his adjutant, who looked over his shoulder and raised himself off his saddle, seeming to find to his liking what he could see.

As the march went on Martin took a look for himself at the trail of men winding down the road. There was excitement at being a part of a whole regiment of his countrymen on the move.

They were in such fine spirits. It did him good to think how he would describe the scene to his family in his next letter. He was glad now he had waited before writing. There would be so much more to tell.

A strong, lusty version of "Mademoiselle from Armentières" worked its way up from the rear, overtaking all other songs in its path. It rang out into the impending night with a bluster that could only lift the spirits even more. Mademoiselle was engaged in rather more carnal activities than in the original verses, but the brass seemed not to care, some even joining in when it suited them.

It was a game and hearty lot that trooped the French countryside toward Acheux-en-Amienois. They called their loads "a bloody nuisance," cutting into their shoulders, and dragging them down, but they managed most of the time to keep it out of their minds.

The return to "Keep the Home Fires Burning" announced to the village their advance. They had gone back to the song again and again, and ever more soberly, it seemed to Hayward. As they marched through, in the near darkness now, a few villagers found time to stand and watch in partially opened doorways. Hayward thought again of Marie-Louise, of her standing by the road, and the look in her eyes as he finally turned away from her.

There was much relief when the colonel called a halt just east of the village. The men dispersed to an open field along the road and quickly dropped their packs. They lay about, smoking, in passive conversation. The colonel and the higher ranks stood together discussing the route they were to take. The men agreed— the longer the talk, the better for all concerned. The going could only get worse.

It was futile to try ignoring what was to be heard coming from the front lines. As the darkness settled down on them, artillery exchanges streaked the eastern sky, in brazen contrast to the stars overhead and the pinpoints of their cigarettes. Most of the men gathered in small groups and turned their attention to themselves. Only a few, the habitual loners, rested with a full view of it all. It was they who spotted again the regiment that had trooped past them in Louvencourt.

"Took the long way 'round, did ya?"

The regiment crossed in front of A Company,

a welcome diversion, and a chance to affirm once again the bond between them, for there were many with friends in the regiment. Now, with the war much closer at hand, the exchanges were mostly sober wishes for luck and good fortune.

"They're over the top before us, I'd say," Moss declared after the last of them had passed.

"That's good," said Martin. "Wouldn't want to be one of the first."

"The others'll have the job done on 'em be then?"

They both looked at Smith, puzzled by his broad smile.

"Don't mind him" said Moss. "He's barmy. The closer to the line, the worse he gets."

Hayward, who had been stopping to talk to one group of men after another, came with a bit of news. "Looks like we'll be here for a while, boys. The colonel's decided it's best to wait till it's darker before setting off again. He doesn't want to take any chances on the Boche getting a look at us crossing over that ridge."

"By God, I'll go along with that," Smith said, loudly. "Tell him, if he wants, we'll camp here for the night."

"I don't say he'd be too keen."

The others chuckled. Martin felt himself
stiffen slightly. It was the darkness covering him
now, the shield against them noticing everything
he did. As the edge of afterglow disappeared
from the sky, he was thankful to draw away into
himself. He liked the distance between them.

The officer who had scouted the new route
earlier in the day was given the lead, and the
order went out for the men to fall in. The formation took shape along the road, without the
precision of the first time, and the march was
set in motion once again, in the direction of
Mailly-Maillet.

It was straight on to it now, and no escap-
ing a flagrant view of where they were headed.
From the distance the rumble and flare ranted
at them, worse than any storm anyone could
remember. They plodded on, into the eye of it.

There was no singing. The chatter that had
punctuated the first miles was gone. Their words
were of necessity, or relief—the wish for a cigarette, the curse that followed a stumble. Their
equipment grew to a hellish torment, with
absolutely nothing to be done about it.

Hayward felt the need to reassure them, get
them to see the strength of their number, a

platoon that would face it together. He moved about, marching along in the dark with some of the men and then others, making certain they all knew he was there.

"That's the stuff, Martin. We'll be settled away for a rest before long."

It seemed to Hayward that the fellow had shown considerable nerve at the start. Yet he had nothing to say. Hayward left it at that. He marched with him for a good distance, and threw out a remark now and then about how much worse it had been in Gallipoli.

When an especially brilliant flash lit the horizon he said it was nothing to some he had witnessed, and from closer quarters. "They'll have them pounded good. What's left won't be enough for target practice."

He offered no explanation when it was the other side's shells raining down. And Martin asked no questions, just kept up a steady pace. It was straight ahead and not a look to left or right.

A harder test came farther on. The regiment topped the hill into Mailly-Maillet, but instead of entering it as the men expected, a route was struck across the open fields to the south. In single file they marched, even the colonel forced to go the rest of the way on foot. Around them rang the thundering boom of heavies slamming the German lines, and up ahead field batteries lashed at their barbed wire.

The countryside was turning to mud and rubble, having been trampled again and again, then ripped to bits by weeks of enemy fire. No one could see any distance except when the shells struck, but the slogging underfoot and the stench wafting over them was evidence enough for any man that the Front had been reached.

"Not long now, lads!"

An officer struck out ahead of them to get the batteries to hold off until the troops passed through. As their pace slowed it was every man to himself. The blasts were security to some— the show of strength only reinforcing what the generals had been preaching all along. Others of them, especially the ones new at the game, shuddered at the intensity and wished to God the line would move faster.

The field batteries ceased and word came down the line that the communication trench had been reached. A boost to them all, to be sure. But short lived. Past the gun positions, the march came to a sudden halt.

Hayward heard the commotion at the entrance to the trench and went in search of Clarke. He knew nothing, but in no time the captain came by.

"Crammed full with another battalion."

"We can't stay out in the open like this, sir."

"You have another solution, Clarke? I'm sure the colonel would love to hear it."

"How long, sir?" Hayward said.

"As long as it takes!" he barked and was gone, down the line to find the other officers.

"How much more are they going to bugger up before it's over?" Clarke said.

Hayward had his watch out but couldn't read it. Clarke crouched in tight to him and scratched a match across a piece of brimstone.

"After midnight." A moment later Hayward added, "The first day of July."

Suddenly, above them, came the swish of enemy shells.

"By God!" blared Clarke.

They landed a good distance away, but caused a hellish commotion throughout the line.

Hayward rushed back to his men.

"I told them to stay calm, sir." The corporal was obviously no calmer than any of the others.

"A hard racket. Nothin' close, though, sir."
It was Smith, who had made his way past several men to get to him.

"With any luck they'll stay that way."

"Nothin' for us to worry about. It's the poor blighters under 'em what's got it bad."

The next shell swooped past their heads, striking the ground not half as far away as the first ones.

"Sir, we can't stay out here! We'll sure as hell get it."

"The colonel is doing what he can!"

The next shell struck to the rear of them.

"Bloody hell! It's D Company, sure enough!"

They were convinced the next shell was marked for them. Hayward tried to calm them down, but nothing he said brought any relief. The wait went on forever.

It wore Martin to the ground. He slumped there, his head in his hands. He had to escape it—the noise, the thick caustic smell, the damn talk. His breath ran short and deep. He locked shut his eyes.

He heard someone call his name and was instantly on his feet.

"Yes, sir. We're moving now, sir?"

"Any minute."

A heavy shell, a Jack Johnson, struck and mud flew at them. Curses ripped the air.

"Easy!" Hayward bellowed.

Finally the line started to move. The men pushed ahead, cramming against each other. It was an eternity getting to Tipperary Avenue, the communication trench, but in the end they made it.

"Hardly a scratch," the captain told them after he got the word. "D Company had to deploy for a time, but every man accounted for. Thank God."

The men felt a good deal better after that. The captain could always be counted on to keep it in perspective.

SEVENTEEN

For some who trudged along there was the knowledge of being on familiar ground, for it had been work parties from the regiment who'd dug a good bit of the trench they were in.

It had been a mud hole a few days before. The duckboards kept them out of most of the muck that remained, yet there was no way to avoid it all.

Smith had taken to whistling a few of the regiment's favourites. Eventually he gave it up, when he could see no one had any intention of joining him. When Bennett pushed past him he came close to making a crack about how a few shells had nearly driven Bennett off his head. But just seeing the corporal with the wind up like a pissass private was plenty to satisfy him.

Smith had made sure young Martin was right in front of him in the push through to the support trench. He hadn't said a word, in spite of Smith's jabbering over the artillery fire, until Smith said something about his father, the customs man, and what he'd be thinking of it all if he could see him now.

"You got no cause to be talkin' about Father," Martin snapped.

"No point to it till we're settled in for the night," Smith said to Moss behind him. "Give the poor young bugger a couple hours' rest after the guns dies down. He'll come around."

The communication trench connected through to St. John's Road, the support trench where the regiment would hold up. It was from there they'd be going over the top.

"Got its name," Moss yelled ahead to Martin, "'cause we fellers worked our guts off. Had to leave it to the South Wales crowd to finish up." He added, "Consider yerself lucky you wasn't 'ere for that. Nothin' worse than diggin' ruddy trenches."

St. John's Road was deeper and wider than Tipperary Avenue, with dugouts, and cubby-holes where a man could have a rest. When he could be heard, Smith blared at the young fellow about what a slog the digging had been and how they'd worked like dogs to fix up parapets and put in traverses.

Martin hadn't a clue what either one of them was going on about. His mind was a jumble. His nerve was hauled to pieces. He dragged on ahead of Smith barely keeping upright with the stop-and-start-again surge through the line. The artillery, every time it thundered off, pounded his head into his shoulders. Keeping to his feet and getting through—there was nothing more to be done.

The trench cut at right angles, like teeth, back and forth, dug that way so if the Boche got in they could never fire their machine-guns straight down the length of it. From the head of the platoon, Hayward yelled back warning of places where shells had smashed into the trench and what had to be done to get past. Like him, his men craved an end to the march.

Not one of them complained. They hadn't the energy any more to waste on it.

EIGHTEEN

I t was two-thirty in the morning when the regiment made it to their sector, the stretch of St. John's Road where they could finally settle in, for whatever was left of the night, and from where they'd be taking the jump over in the morning. It was 250 yards to their own front lines. And at least five hundred more to the trenches of the dirty blackguards who were putting them through this hell.

The first thing to do was rid themselves of their packs. Not a man in the section spoke. The relief at finally making it twisted in their guts.

Word came along that the brass had given the okay to light up, and the section to a man searched out a fag. It was welcome almost as much as the halt in the march. They slumped where there was space to be found, on their packs most of them, and took some comfort in knowing they were all together still. A couple of men dared to remove their tin hats, letting the night air cool their heads.

Smith began to whistle something quiet and slow. The others paid little mind, figuring it another army tune. But between the shelling overhead, the old ode to the Island could be heard. In time all the section joined in on bits of it, though it never seemed to rise any louder, and eventually it trailed off as quietly as it had started. Not a man said a word.

Hayward came by, breaking the silence. He assigned sentry duty, a half hour each man. That would give them all a fair chance at some sleep, not that sleep was going to come to any of them very easily. Moss was happy enough to be the first one and getting it over with right away.

"Have an eye, now, Moss. No poking at them rations."

"Me, sir? Not a blink, sir."

Hayward was off to the other sections. Eventually, he weaved his way half-blindly through the trench in an effort to find Clarke. He came across him hard at it, trying to straighten out one of his men on using a latrine.

It was good reason for Clarke to be finished with it. He followed Hayward. "Did it on the other fellow's foot, by God. Too dark. Couldn't see!"

They headed to where they could expect to find the captain. Getting past the other sections in the dark of the trench again proved a confounded business. Several times they had to root at exhausted men to get them out of the way, and at one turn up jumped a surly private, to discover just in time whose foot had jabbed him in the ribs.

Finally, they reached what they thought would be the captain's dugout. Clarke recalled the spot from the times he had directed trench-digging parties. They bent their heads and proceeded along a tunnel to its entrance. It was covered by a blanket, but shafts of dim light outlined its edges.

The room was one of the better ones, as Clarke had remembered, with a platform against one wall for a bed, and big enough to hold a table and a few crates for seats. The stub of a candle burnt on the table. The captain sat on the edge of the bed, checking his pistol. He had already made the place home, with the brass-framed photograph of his family that he took with him wherever he went. To Hayward and Clarke he appeared particularly odd in the uniform of the ordinary soldier.

He caught their looks. "The first one they came up with was even bigger," he said.

"It's not the size, sir," Hayward said. "You've always been an officer, since I can remember, even in the Methodist Guards."

"The Hun'll have the devil's own time figuring who to shoot at," said Clarke.

Myers came through the curtain. "Another young tommy," said Clarke. "This'll even out your chances, Wilf."

The comment was lost on him. He had serious matters on his mind that he was desperate to bring to the captain's attention.

"The colonel's been in touch with Brigade, sir. It's coming through well enough. The shelling doesn't seem to have damaged the lines any."

"What's the word from the major-general?"

He hesitated. "I wouldn't know, sir." There was a prolonged pause. "The colonel wants the company commanders to be aware that everything is under control."

The captain went back to checking his pistol.

"Very well," he said when it suited him.

"I'll be off, then, sir."

"Get some sleep," he said, without looking up.

Myers was gone.

"A lot on his mind," Clarke said, in a tone that Hayward knew at once would not be to the captain's liking.

"What do you have on *your* mind, Mr. Clarke?"

Hayward interrupted. "We wanted to let you know the men are no worse for the march." There was silence. "Including Pendergast."

"I expected they would be."

"I'd say the Jack Johnsons did a first-rate job sobering him up," Clarke said.

"Anything you need us to do, sir? We thought we'd check."

The captain looked directly into their faces for the first time. "Talk to the men. Get some sleep. Wait. What more is there?" He put the pistol in its leather case and looked at them again.

Shadows flickered about the walls as the two of them turned to go. A rat scurried across the floor. Clarke instantly made a swipe at it with his boot, missing the rat but striking one of the crates, upending it. He returned the crate to its place, smiled at the captain and left, just ahead of Hayward.

The shelling had died down considerably. The air was cold and thick, like that from wet, dirty flannel. Finding a place to catch some sleep was the worst of it. The men could put up with the chill and the trench smells, but there had proved to be more bodies than places for them to lie. A lucky few had claimed what firesteps and dry platforms there were, but most had to be content to wait their turn for a spot or try to sleep sitting up.

When he reached his men Hayward discovered most of them had given up on the prospect of sleep and were huddled together, smoking and talking. They wondered if he brought any news, especially anything about the colonel and what he thought of the way the regiment had stood up so far.

"First rate, as far as I can tell. Brigade says everything's primed to go."

"I'd say the colonel's happy enough. He knows he's got a swarm o' keeners."

"Lyin' back in hes dugout, I'd say, havin' a grand old nip to keep warm."

The speculation made the round, though

there was no envy in their voices. None among the lot cared to be the one to send them into whatever lay beyond the lip of trench.

Martin added his bit. "I'd say he's wishing for fog."

"He'll have to do more than wish," said Moss. "Now if we could haul up and shift the whole bloody works to Cape Bonavist', no tellin' what might come of it. The Hun could be lost in the fog for a week."

"End up on an ice floe and never be heard tell of again, what."

Martin chuckled along with them. He was feeling pretty steady now. A lot of it was Smith's doing, he'd admit that, but maybe the worst of it was past. There was all kinds of talk about what the artillery had put over in the last week, and that the regiment might just walk straight to the lines and not fire a shot.

He could picture that. And wouldn't it be a fine sight, and how proud they'd all look, marching straight on then to Beaumont Hamel.

It was the encroaching night chill that tormented him most. He had to put up with mud-soaked boots and puttees, and the waterproof sheet that was wrapped around his upper body did little to keep out the cold. The only source of heat was his breath, and a cigarette that he kept cupped in his hands, even when he brought it to his lips for a draw.

His body ached for sleep, but he had to slump against the trench wall, no position for his head except hanging forward or to one side. And there was too much churning through it, too many possible situations to fix in his mind. He looked at Smith next to him nodding off and wondered how it was at all that the man could sleep.

The best he could do for himself was to think about home. The four girls wouldn't stop talking about him, that was certain. His mother would go on and on and maybe she'd forgive his father for ever letting him go. They'd have so many questions, all of them. He'd tell his father just what a hell it was and his father would have to bring him along in his uniform to the customs office to talk to the men. He'd want them to know the worst of it.

Hayward came by and shared a cigarette with him. All the time Martin was thinking how he'd never have predicted the two of them would be in it together. Some evenings, when the war was over, they'd get together in the parlour and tell stories and smoke the expensive cigars that his father bargained for off the foreign boats. His father might bring out a bottle of Jamaican rum, the best he had, and the night would be full of stories his father could hardly believe.

"Never mind, Ned, we'll have our laughs over this one yet," Hayward whispered.

Martin nodded.

"Don't you be worrying. The artillery boys got a lot more of the heavy stuff for the Hun to chew on."

"That girl, is she yours?" he asked, as if he hadn't heard a word.

Hayward changed position.

"I saw her on the roadside. I had a girl of my own once."

"What was her name?"

"Rose."

"Did you love her?"

"I was mad for her. Then she started seeing some damn quiff from Patrick Street."

"There'll be others," Hayward said.

"Do you love yours, then?"

"Yes."

"Will you see her again?"

"As soon as I can."

Neither spoke. The night chill stiffened them. For a few seconds there lingered a heavy, black silence, as if nothing anywhere was moving. In a corner of the trench a man coughed. From farther along another could be heard, urinating.

The wait gnawed at them. In the dark Hayward had his moments of dread, though he forced them aside and pushed on with his business. He had been holding off on a weapons inspection in favour of uninterrupted sleep for the men, but now he worked his way along the trench, rousing each of them in turn.

He found much of it a useless exercise, what with the darkness and the lousy conditions. At most he came away reasonably certain they'd kept their Lee-Enfields out of the mud. They all seemed to have their correct supply of ammunition and, as far as he could tell, the Mills bombs had survived the march intact. He'd always trusted his men to keep their firearms in good order and never had they let him down. When daylight came, checking their rifles would be the first thing every one of them would do.

Smith was the last of the lot. Hayward made only a cursory check. The fellow had been through more than enough to know the consequences of a weapon that jammed. Besides, he was one of the few actually sleeping.

"Get it while you can," he said, lifting off his tin hat and scraping his head with his thick fingers. "If there's no more than lice and rats crawlin' over me 'fore the day is over …"

"What do you think, Smith?"

"Ah, I give up thinkin'." He spat on the duck-boards.

Hayward waited him out.

"Hard to say, sir. Foolish, a lot of it. Fritz is not stupid. Maybe they're dug in deep. The regiments what's over 'fore us, they'll find out soon enough."

"We can only hope for the best." Hayward realized as soon as it came out that it was a poor thing to be saying.

Moss had overheard them. He piped up, "Dug in deep and ready for a hammering."

"Mossie's all set, aren't ya, Mossie?"

"Like the bird," came the voice out of the dark.

Smith chuckled. "Always like the bird."

The corporal came by. Hayward had noticed that he'd been going about the trench with rather less of a head on him than before.

"Probably, sir, we should be issuing the rest

of the battle stores any time now."

"I've been wondering when that bloomin' trench bridge was goin' to show hes face," said Moss. "Too roomy here for my likin'."

"That so?" said Bennett, who didn't find the least bit of humour in it. He continued as if only Hayward was there. "I can take care of it, sir."

"You do that."

The heavier of the battle stores—the trench ladders and bridges, the bangalore torpedoes— were in the trenches when the men arrived, sent ahead by transport. It was a matter of sorting out what lot belonged to each section. The corporal and a private he had commandeered for the job saw to it that every piece made it to its rightful owner.

When Hayward checked to be certain they all could handle their loads, the first thing he came up against was the matter of Moss's trench bridge. The fellow was bound and determined there'd be some kind of foul-up when the time came to go over the top.

"It's you and Smith. And you won't hear another word about it."

He found the corporal prone on a firestep, trying in vain to sleep. Hayward told him straight away what he'd done, and how he was sure it was for the best, given what he knew of the pair. "It's different out there. They've got to have each other."

To his surprise, the corporal showed no concern. He seemed to expect it. As far as Hayward could tell, he was far from the trenches for the moment. Out of his tunic pocket he took an envelope and placed it in Hayward's hand.

"Will you take this, sir? I think it'll be safer with you."

Hayward said nothing, and did not move his hand.

"I have a feeling it will, sir. It's for my aunt. She'll need something."

His aunt in St. George's was the only relative he ever talked about. Hayward had wondered about his parents, but never asked.

"It'll be no safer with me."

"I have to be sure it gets to her."

"It will." He placed the envelope back in the corporal's hand.

After a moment it was returned to his tunic pocket. "You won't forget it's there?"

"Can't think I would."

"I want to thank you, sir."

Hayward left the corporal with a few words about trying to get more sleep.

It was advice that he might have heeded himself if he hadn't long ago accepted that there was no way of him getting any on the eve of an attack. The best he could do was find a place to keep dry and hope there was something that could take his mind off it.

Even the rats were a welcome diversion. The trench rats in France were big enough that Hayward mistook the first one he saw for a cat. Their brazenness under cover of night was just as notorious. It came as no surprise, when he settled down, that one crawled from the parapet sandbags to have a crack at a piece of shortbread biscuit he had just removed from his haversack.

"Bloody rogue," he hissed, taking a swipe at the rat and just missing the private who stirred beside him.

"Was it ration, sir?"

"From home. The last one."

"Kill the bugger."

It was the last piece of shortbread from the package he'd received in the mail a few days before. Stale now, but still, something from home. The theft of a ration biscuit he might have abided (or welcomed, as the private said), but this was an insult not to be taken lightly. He unleashed his disgust with a verbal blast unmatched by any of his previous encounters with the rodents.

"Well now, sir, I never heard you get on like that before," the private remarked. "Not that the dirty blighter didn't deserve it, mind you."

Hayward laughed. The captain would have thought him a fool and called it unbefitting an officer, though he cared not a damn.

NINETEEN

One of Clarke's men came through the darkness calling his name. Hayward followed him back to some place that might have passed for the dugout it was meant to be had it not been smacked by a shell and never properly repaired.

He entered by the light of a candle burning atop the rubble in one corner. Clarke, however, had been able to make the place livable. In fact, he was stretched out royally on a ground sheet, his body curved at an odd angle to avoid a collapsed beam. His head rested against one hand; a panatella protruded between the fingers of the other.

"Is this safe?" said Hayward, looking upward.

"Safe? My man, when all around us looms

the dreaded unknown?"

Hayward stood in a crouch a few seconds longer, then sat down on a piece of broken plank.

"I have a proposition."

Hayward was leery of asking.

"It's a damned fine proposition, really." He smiled. He waited, though he knew Hayward was not about to say anything. "It concerns a certain possibility."

He took another draw of his panatella, then passed it to Hayward with a sweep of his hand. "If, perchance … and no one seems to have any idea of the likelihood … but nevertheless, if it should happen that both of us get it … shall we say wounded …"

"Shouldn't you be a bit more of a stalwart, Clarke? How did you actually spend your time in officer training?"

Clarke was amused for the moment. He continued, "If it should, then let's have a pact—you won't try being the hero to help me, and I'll forgo the medal and let the stretcher-bearers do their job on you."

Hayward suddenly resented what he was seeing beneath the mock propriety. Why in hell's name get on like that? What good did it do anyone? He said as much with the look he gave him.

"No sweating it, chum," Clarke said, "if that's the way you want it. Just trying to make it easier for the both of us."

"You've got a damn nerve."

"As much as I need to play the game."

"I've been through as much as you have."

"Good for you. What about it—what name have you got for this one?"

"Not me, Clarke. Where the hell does it all get you?"

"Nowhere that you're not going, chum."

"Why go on with it, then?"

"I've asked myself that very question. Many times. I don't take to being told not to ask questions. That much I've concluded."

"I do, I suppose?"

"I'm no closer to the answer, if that says anything."

Hayward swore at the way Clarke had taken him on. He got to his feet.

"Allan, have a drink," Clarke said, in a tone as dispassionate as before. "Brandy. I was going to save it till after the show."

Hayward left without a word. Outside the dugout he came to a sudden stop. He found a spot against the trench wall, oblivious of the men scattered all about. Why make it worse now? Why couldn't Clarke keep his cursed notions to himself?

Hayward stayed there long enough that, in the end, he took it as Clarke's way, as he'd done all the other times. He went back into the dugout.

On the ground in front of Clarke, unopened, was the small silver flask, scratched and dented so much that Clarke's initials were no longer discernible. Hayward had never seen him take it out in anyone else's presence, and had often seen him conceal it when a third officer came their way.

Hayward sat where he had before. He reached for the flask and put it to his lips without looking at Clarke. He had a gulp and placed it back on the ground. The liquor stung his throat and burnt the chill from his insides. "I try not to think of her," he said. "Marie-Louise. She's a wonderful girl. I should have had you meet her."

Clarke lifted the flask as if he was making a toast.

"I miss her," Hayward said. "She'll still be there."

His friend took a long drink, then put the

flask away. After a while his head slipped from his hand and Hayward watched as his eyes closed and he seemed to fall asleep.

For a long time Hayward remained there, in the same position, watching the candlelight, and letting the longed-for silence of the night settle in his head.

TWENTY

Martin stirred. He had no way of knowing if he had fallen asleep. It was the silence that roused him, he thought as he worked his neck from side to side to get the stiffness out. It was the quietest it had been since their leaving Louvencourt. There was little to be heard except the shifting about of the man on sentry duty.

Even Smith had quieted down. At the time Martin couldn't believe he was snoring. Moss had poked him in the ribs with the butt of his rifle, and it hadn't been heard since.

Martin blamed the cold, as much as anything, for the misery that encased him. He felt he was clay heaped against the trench wall, with the expectation of it coming to life at dawn, somehow ready to do what had to be done. He had no urge to do anything but stay where he was. He shut his eyes and returned to the words of prayers that had started to muddle about again in his head.

They were displaced by Hayward's voice at his side. Martin had not heard him approach, and neither did it register at first who it might be. Only when Hayward said something about the Brennan boys on Maxse Street did he open his eyes and lift his head.

"Forever down on the waterfront, aboard the schooners. I can see 'em now—straight up the rigging and not think twice about it."

"Foolhardy, Mother used to call 'em," Martin said. "Said they'd have their necks cracked if they wasn't careful."

"Joined the navy, I expect."

"Slackers. Worst of the lot. Father told 'em as much to their faces."

Hayward moved away. Martin realized he had other things to occupy him. Though when Hayward did return, following a few words to the man on sentry duty, Martin was relieved.

They waited out the dawn together.

TWENTY-ONE

It came like a secret murmured from a great distance, growing slowly louder and louder. Over the land rose the mist, vapour oozing from the scarred fields, its tendrils lurking in the stagnant shell-hole waters, undraping a battleground that seemed reluctant to show itself.

In the trenches the blackness turned a thick, murky grey. Shadowy figures stirred, shifted about uneasily and settled back again. As the break of day thinned the gloom, the fitfulness spread, and the mutterings of men stiff with the cold began to swell.

With the light came the renewed charge of shelling overhead, lest anyone had been lulled into forgetting all that surrounded them. There was no time to linger with thoughts of what might not be. Instead came the stir of blood renewing their limbs, the rousing of their hearts to contempt for the devils on the other side of no man's land.

For most it came as a relief from the sleeplessness and the insufferable wait through the night. Light permeated the depths of the trenches, enough finally that they could make out with some certainty who had settled where. The men came to life, eager to rid themselves of the thoughts that overnight had clogged their heads, like so much bric-a-brac from their youth.

Now was set an even stronger urge to get on with it. They filled some of the time checking their equipment. The Lee-Enfields were foremost for attention, getting as much as the light would allow. Their rifles they gripped with determination, certain it would revive any of the vigorous confidence that might have waned overnight.

The battle stores assigned during the night showed themselves to be even more ungainly appendages than they had imagined. It suddenly occurred to some how great the task to get up and over the lip of the trench. It could not be the fleet-footed vault to action they had demonstrated time after time in training.

They would make it, nonetheless. There could never be any doubt about that. For now, they sat and smoked and let the dawn uncover more of what had been their home for the several hours past.

Martin, for one, did not care to see the shield of darkness lifted away, revealing, as it did, his sunken frame. He straightened up, and resisted the urge to vacantly ignore those around him, every one of whom, it seemed to him, was brighter than they had any good reason to be.

Why the need to be so heedlessly cheerful? Yet he could not have them think he was anything other than their equal. He looked about and chuckled and they noticed nothing of his private moments when his hands tightened one into the other.

It was Smith only who saw the lameness in his motions. The fellow came over with a fagend in his outstretched hand. Martin refused it, though he moved aside in case Smith was wanting a spot next to him, now that Hayward had gone.

"Take what comes and be glad it's no worse."

"For God's sake, don't be telling me how bad

ye fellows had it in Gallipoli."

Smith broke out laughing, though it was lost in a roar of artillery fire. The others added to it. For what reason, Martin was at odds to know, for they couldn't have heard what he'd said.

"This haze'll burn off 'fore you know it. No rain, bud, you can bet on that."

Martin wasn't paying any mind now. "Never let you down, not Shep. She's a wonderful mutt," he said. "She is, too, the best kind."

"You'll do fine, bud."

Martin wouldn't do much more than look for the moment into his face, then rub both hands together, as Smith was doing, to generate some heat.

"You'll have to come by and see her," Martin said, raising his voice. "Not home. It'll be too much of a commotion with the girls. It'd give Mother one of her headaches. She wouldn't want to hear any of your stories, that's for certain. We'd go somewhere and have us an ale or two. She needn't know, sure."

"We'll have to see, bud."

Bennett appeared, with orders for everyone to stand-to at once.

Martin was on his feet immediately, as if the

Hun were about to show up in their hundreds. Smith might have found it funny had the young fellow not been so deadly serious in getting into position on the firestep. Smith told him to save his steam for the real thing.

Yet there was no slacking off. He remained stiff, his rifle poised in anticipation of some fool leaping over the edge of the trench at any minute.

Only when Bennett snapped out something about the way he was holding his rifle did the spell break.

Martin turned and, with pure loathing, glared at the corporal. He waited for a break in the artillery fire.

"You've got dogshit in your eyes, sir."

Martin turned back calmly to face the trench wall again, leaving the corporal stunned. The man moved in a daze to the next fire bay and out of sight, as if nothing had happened, as if it had all been a misunderstanding.

Smith could barely hold it in and, on the next roar of artillery, blew out laughing. Straightaway he passed the story on to Moss, who howled and slapped his leg.

It all brought a weak smile to the young fellow, whose mind was fixed still on the whereabouts of the enemy, and on some place far off, where one day, he was thinking, he'd be another one of the men back from the war.

TWENTY-TWO

The sun drew away from the artillery fire vying stubbornly with it for attention along the horizon. It rose free of the smoke and haze to shine with equal brilliance on all the trenches. As it did so, the British artillery bombardment swelled, until it became a wild, unceasing tumult.

When the captain peered through the periscope over the lip of trench near his dugout, what he saw was the flash of light against his own barbed wire. From that angle he could not make out the British front line, though he knew it to be there. Just as he knew beyond the fourth belt of wire was no man's land, and somewhere beyond that, where the land sloped away, was the German wire, and the Germans in their trenches.

He could not find many gaps in the wire, yet he shouted to the company's officers, who had joined him, that the gaps had to be there. They each had a quick look and nodded in agreement. All but Clarke.

Clarke held back even when they were hunched together in the dugout afterward, about to go over for a final time how the attack was to unfold. His reserve was of more interest than any of what was being said, since they had heard every detail dozens of times before.

Their job would be to occupy the enemy's third line of trenches, following the advance of the 87th Brigade—the South Wales Borderers at zero hour, 7:30, and the King's Own Scottish Borderers and the Border Regiment at 8:05. The Newfoundland, and the Essex on their right, would lead their 88th Brigade over the top at 8:40, the third wave of the attack.

The captain pointed to the Puisieux Trench on the map, their objective. The 87th would have done their job on the Germans in the first two trench lines, and, as Headquarters was saying, the blighters would be in such confusion the 88th might never have to fire a shot. The regiment had five thousand yards of ground to cover, so that hardly seemed likely, even to the most optimistic of the lot standing around the map.

Clarke continued to look on in silence. Even the arrival of Myers, direct from the colonel's dugout, was not enough to break it. Clarke flashed Hayward a look. It seemed Myers's agitated movement about the trenches was enough to convince the others his role was vital to the whole operation. He had been ordered to Brigade Headquarters to synchronize watches, and on his return the colonel sent him to make a quick round of the companies. Myers laid out the all-important watch on the map and each of the officers in turn took it up and set his own watch to it.

Hayward removed his from his breeches pocket and immediately he thought of his father. In his next letter he would tell him what importance the watch had taken on. He looked at it lying in his hand, for a moment admiring its sturdiness, then with more care than he had taken any time before, he set it to the exact time.

Myers had no hesitation making known his latest brush with the higher-ups. He was keen to relay that Headquarters was "top-notch" and "never more confident than what it is right now."

Hayward caught Clarke's eye. He hated to see Clarke with that look, as if it was only a matter of time before he would be proved right. At least when he spoke his mind there were plenty who didn't hesitate to have it out with him.

Myers was gone from the dugout as quickly as he had entered. His appearance had given the others a glimpse of the whole show, the orders fixed in place from one end of the line to the other, the thousands of men primed to spring at the whistles, the Newfoundland one link in the chain of regiments stretched for miles through the valley of the Somme.

And not for a second did the captain let them forget that their job was of equal importance to that of any regiment. There was not one officer about to see the Newfoundland Regiment shown up by any other, no matter what might await them when they poured out of the trenches.

That, more than anything, Hayward figured, was what was keeping Clarke quiet. And so it should, he thought.

"Everything clear, gentlemen?" the captain called out, loud enough to be heard above the roar from outside. He began to fold the map back into its leather casing.

"Yes, sir."

"Questions?" He put the map into the breast pocket of his tunic with a decisiveness that suggested there shouldn't be any.

No one spoke. He looked directly at Clarke. "Good."

There was a hesitancy to move off, though each knew the time had come. It was Clarke who turned first to go.

"Gentlemen!" the captain said. "Good luck!"

Hayward thought, another captain might have had a flask to raise in the air and pass around.

"Good luck it is," said Clarke. "Until again we meet, wherever that may be." He didn't bother to see if anyone heard him.

He was out into the trench and gone a considerable distance before Hayward caught up with him. The noise was deafening, all the explosions fused into one almighty rumble, like a never-ending wave thundering ashore.

Clarke stopped suddenly and gripped Hayward's hand, looking him straight in the eye, a stare of grudging resignation. Beyond it Hayward could still see much he had come to like about the man. The look gave way to a wrinkling of the eyes and a mouth twisted into a smirk.

Their grip of each other's hands tightened. They might have embraced had there not been others around them. Clarke patted Hayward stiffly on the shoulder, with a "good-bye, chum" loudly in his ear, and was gone, on to his platoon, without looking back.

Hayward watched him disappear and wondered whether that would be the last he would see of him before the whistle.

Hayward arrived in the midst of his men to find them gulping down a hot breakfast. The field kitchens had been given orders to get food to the men before the attack, but he wouldn't have been surprised if they had never made it through. He spied Williams and quickly retrieved the lid of his mess tin. Williams dished him out some tea from the dixie. Tea, with lots of sugar, and a few dry biscuits was all he wanted.

"Ah, sir." They were the only words Hayward could make out. No matter. The fellow was his irrepressible self despite the slog it must have been to get there.

"Good man," Hayward yelled his way, and give him a nod of approval.

As Hayward drank down his tea, he thought of his mother in the kitchen at home. He could not see her face. He could see only the flurry about the kitchen, the need to get him all the food he would eat.

He turned abruptly to his men, who stood sipping their tea, warming their hands with the heat of the containers. How resilient they looked, in spite of the thunderous noise. He saw in their eyes a stiffness of will that reawakened his pride in how far they had come in the last few months. Their good humour was hardly to be believed, poking fun at one another with gestures when words were of no use. This was the real thick of it now. How could his heart be anywhere but with them at every moment?

The corporals fixed their watches by his. He worked his way along the trench, letting it be known that everything was set to go as planned, reassuring his men with his presence. They'd been trained to follow at the word of a leader, as he had been trained to lead. Never could he deny them what was expected.

He turned the corner and encountered Martin slumped on the edge of a firestep. He straightened up when he realized who was standing over him. His stare was that of a man pushed by the ceaseless slam of artillery into a world of his own.

Hayward gave him a good-natured cuff against the shoulder. It did something to bring Martin to life. "Heave it off, Private." Though there was an edge of a smile on Hayward's face, his look said he was expecting better of the lad. He moved on.

The jolt gradually stiffened Martin upright and had him looking left and right at the other men. He saw in their eyes that they were no less tormented than he by the incessant hammering. He would not have them think wrong of him. He would not be cringing from the noise.

Smith gave him a nod and handed him his cigarette. The young fellow sucked at it eagerly, so much so he started to cough, and only stopped himself after he cleared his throat and spat. The others snatched the moment for relief. Their laughter was mute and Martin took no offence.

Indeed, after a few moments, a crooked grin broke across his face. He began to laugh himself, and did so with abandon, jerking his head back to let loose, even though nothing could be heard above the roar.

He tried to steady himself after, when they were all still looking at him. His limbs quaked, though by fits and starts, and with persistence he was able to keep control. The race of images inside his head had slowed to a nagging few, that of home and his school buddies and their football matches in Bannerman Park in the summer's sun. He opened his eyes wider and held to the looks his soldier chums were giving him, managing a calmer smile, a stoutness of will that would not have him give in to it again.

Smith kept an eye to him, and Moss, too. He knew they were there when he needed someone. And he wouldn't have them thinking he couldn't stand up to it. He held tightly to his rifle, in expectation that the bombardment had to soon subside.

Then came the order to stand-to. Martin took quickly to his feet and had them firmly planted on the firestep, his rifle at the ready.

"Zero hour, fifteen minutes!" Bennett shouted, as though it might settle them down.

Their thoughts ran to the South Wales lads in the front trenches. What was waiting over the top for them? And what would still be there later, when their own whistle blew?

And suddenly, hurricane bombardment—its noise an even more incredible pitch—piled on the weight already pounding down on the men just when it seemed there could be nothing new for the artillery to throw over.

The astounding torrent continued, without pause. Martin glanced at the corporal, whose eyes were fixed to his watch in anticipation of what was coming next.

As soon as Bennett looked up, the ground a thousand yards to the left of them burst apart with a massive explosion. Tons of mud and rock spewed skyward, a fearsome cloud of earth, to fall back all about a huge crater. Hawthorn Redoubt had blown, precisely at 7:20.

The shock waves struck the length of St. John's Road, jolting the lines of men standing-to. There had been rumours of a big explosion, but it was only the officers who weren't surprised at just how big it had been. The men resumed their positions, fearless optimism showing in many faces. They were more certain than ever that the last hour had flattened the Hun beyond recovery.

It was but a few minutes to zero hour. The bombardment eased. It was almost as if the whole battleground were pausing to draw a breath. Hayward walked among his men, reinforcing what he saw in their faces, all the time keeping an eye to his watch, wondering what the Germans were able to do now that there could no longer be any doubts an attack was about to rise from the front trenches.

The men near him scrutinized every flicker of his expression, as anxious as he to know the exact moment the Great Push would start. Shellfire still echoed in their ears, joined by a smattering of the real thing. They held their breath as he slipped his watch into his pocket.

From somewhere, ahead of them, there came the sound of a whistle. The noise of a clammering over the parapets.

The shout and rush of the first wave. Zero hour had come.

Now gunfire. The distant rattle of gunfire. Machine-guns.

Not one of the Newfoundlanders moved.

"Is it?"

"Not so."

But they all knew there was no mistaking

the sound. The Hun were having at the South Wales lads. Just how bad, there was no way of telling. But each time the machine-gun fire stopped there were only a few seconds before it started again.

"God," said another of them, gripping the shoulder of the man next to him.

"We expected some," Hayward said. "We were thinking it might be hard going for the first ones."

"You're supposin' that be the worst of it, sir?"

Hayward could not give him an answer.

"The artillery, they'll soon take care of 'em," Smith said.

Hayward drew out his watch. To be sure, right on time, the artillery started up again. Smith nodded approvingly. Hayward did not have the heart to tell him that the artillery's orders were to advance their barrage one hundred yards every two minutes. Certainly, Hayward thought, if the attack was not going right, the major-general would send new orders straight away, and keep the Hun pinned in their trenches.

Hayward directed his men to stand down. There was an hour still before their own time to go. They had never expected it to be easy, yet none was ready for the constant jab of gunfire, and the desperate wait for an end to it.

Most sat on the firesteps or leaned against the trench wall, their tin hats tipped back from their dirt-black faces, their eyes shrunken holes. Mud covered the uniforms, and the boots and puttees were thickly caked with the stuff—all the makings of trench foot, with no point in scraping at any of it. The packs and extra stores made it an even sorrier state of affairs, though there was no complaining. From time to time someone wiped his mouth with the back of a dirty hand and took a swallow from his water bottle. The waiting had to be the worst of it.

They drew more and more into themselves. They forced into their minds the plans they had for when it was over, holding them there as long as they could.

It was Myers tearing by on his way to the captain that snatched their attention. The man was in a hellfire hurry, his eyes fixed dead ahead of him, acknowledging no one. He went past so quickly Hayward was a few seconds realizing just who it had been.

Hayward was on the run after him, uncertain that he even wanted to know the reason for his panic. Myers had no intention of stopping, even when Hayward caught up with him and grabbed his arm. He shoved Myers into the entrance of a dugout.

"You don't have to know."

"What is it?"

"Out of the way."

Hayward didn't move. "You were in the front line? The colonel sent you to synchronize watches?"

He didn't deny it.

"What did you see?"

"Have faith, Allan." His eyes would not focus on him.

"Tell me, Wilf. I'll not have you play the fool with me."

"It'll do you no good."

"Tell me, damn you!"

Myers recoiled. "I was heading back just when the whistle blew," he stammered. "I saw them go over, right ready for it." He drew a laboured breath. "Some dragged themselves back."

"They got it bad?"

He struggled for more words. "The stretcher-bearers, they're on the way."

"The rest kept going?"

"There were so many. Some had to get

through. There couldn't be any stopping them."

Myers slipped past Hayward. He stumbled on and disappeared from sight.

Hayward stood silent, motionless except for one hand in an absent-minded search for his watch. His head rested for a few seconds against the trench wall. He looked at the watch. Their attack was less than fifty minutes away.

He returned to the men, all the time thinking how it must be with the Border Regiment and the King's Own, set to go next. He said nothing of his encounter with Myers, though some had to be expecting it, the way they kept their eyes on him.

Smith did not relent. He continued to stare after the others had given up. His insistence on confronting him, his look asserting he had earned a right to know, drove Hayward to the next fire bay.

Smith turned to Martin. "We'll show the bloody Kaiser what we're made of, you and me and Mossie! There'll be no stopping us. We'll have at the lousy bastards!"

There was enemy gunfire still to be heard between the clamour of artillery, but Smith's ballyhoo turned it to a continuous roar, an unearthly chorus of the man and the stuff of war. Martin was lost in the sheer intensity of it. Moss looked on, laughing to himself, it seemed to the others. They were three of them together, and when the time came, they'd haul each other through.

TWENTY-THREE

Hayward checked his watch. At any moment the other two regiments would be going over. He waited, his ears strained. It came, in far-off bursts between the artillery fire, like knife points striking his chest.

He stiffened and cast off anything the men might take for alarm. Yet he could feel suspicion rising inside him, Clarke's unrelenting stare wedging itself into his conscience.

He reassured his men that the brass had everything in hand. For the regiment was next to go. In less than half an hour it would be them rushing from the trenches.

"Not worried, are you, sir?"

Some of it couldn't help but show. He rid

himself of it with a half-smile and a turn of his head. "There won't be much left in our way. We'll have our go."

His words held no promise, and had no effect. The men were doing what they could to shrug off the anxiety, as each crack of gunfire wore into them. Any eagerness for what the day would bring subsided, though their spirit remained. A true man of the regiment would never see that go.

When the word came again to stand-to, they took to the firesteps with renewed intensity. It would be straight into it and no holding back. the reputation of the regiment was theirs to be made. The fight was what mattered, and they'd have their crack at the Hun, and see the dirty cowards crawl back into their holes.

The minutes went by, their passing marked in sonorous tones by the corporal. He had decided such a count was necessary, and Hayward left him to it. At least it put a stop to the fellow's incessant wandering about the trench.

At 8:20 it all came to a sudden halt.

"From the colonel, sir," the runner said, without stopping. "Stand by until further orders." He eyed Hayward long enough to be sure he was the one in charge, and was gone.

The men looked at each other and then at Hayward.

They took their old spots, many sitting shoulder to shoulder on the firesteps. It came as no relief, just a longer wait, and now with more doubts about how the other regiments had fared.

It was Smith who put the best face on it. "Maybe there's nothin' left to do, sir. Maybe the lads got the job done for us."

There was no one taking hold of that, especially when a few seconds later the sound of machine-gun fire drifted over them again. Even Smith fell silent.

Hayward took a look at Martin. The lad sat with his rifle upright between his knees, holding it with both hands, his mind somewhere else. Hayward lit a cigarette and held it out to him. Martin did not notice at first, and when he did, he shook his head.

"Mother wouldn't like it, sir."

The men were mute and as impenetrable as Hayward had ever seen them. He could not abide it.

He would go and search out Clarke.

Within a couple of minutes he came upon

him, standing about with his men. Clarke showed
no surprise and led him toward the dugout.

"What do you make of it? Tell me," Hayward
burst out before they were inside.

In the semi-darkness Clarke lit a panatella,
the last he had, he told Hayward. He blew out
the smoke and stared at his friend.

"Hell, Clarke."

"Obviously, you don't think it's so good."

"You do?"

"When has my opinion made any difference?"

"Bloody hell."

"The poor bastards."

"Machine-guns, they've not stopped."

"I crawled over the lip for a look," Clarke said.

Hayward could hardly think it true.

"They had too many other targets to pay any
notice. I had to find out."

The silence confirmed everything Hayward
feared.

"One of the damn guns is right where
Hawthorn blew." He took a long draw. "The brass
saying ten minutes was not going to make any
difference. Bloody fools."

Hayward looked toward Clarke's men. "What
did you tell them?"

"Nothing. No point."

"Maybe the Welsh boys are getting through now?"

"You can hope."

"They won't send our lads out in it, then. There'll be no reason."

Clarke said nothing.

"They'll pull back the field batteries and put up a barrage."

"Would you count on it?"

Hayward had struck a wall. "So we sit and wait?" he spat out. "Leave it up to them?"

"That's it."

Clarke took a last draw on the panatella, all the time staring at Hayward.

"Damn you, Clarke!"

Clarke did not move, nor change his expression. "One star on the tunic cuff, remember."

"We'll go to the captain."

"The dear captain, forever open to advice."

"He'll listen to me, damn it. Crawl back in a hole, if that's what you want. Bloody hell, Clarke!"

"Bloody hell, is it."

But Hayward had gone. Clarke's eyes shut for a moment.

He chased after Hayward and caught up

before he'd gone far. They made their way past the men without a look or a word to each other.

Just before turning the corner to where they had last seen the captain, Hayward stopped. He turned to Clarke. "When I was about to join up, the captain told my father he didn't think I'd make it as a soldier. Didn't think I had the nerve for it."

They found the captain by himself in the dugout. He could have been praying, Hayward thought when he first set eyes on him sitting there, his hands between his knees.

"Sir," said Hayward.

"You two should be with your men!"

"Will they have the regiment go over still? It's not good, is it, sir?"

"Who are you to say what's not good?"

"The machine-guns. We know the Welsh lads—"

"What is it you know, Hayward?" he barked. "You were there? You saw something with your own eyes?"

"I saw it," Clarke interrupted.

"Get back to your men, Clarke." He glared at him, dismissing out of hand anything he was about to add. "And you're to stay there until we get the word from Brigade. You don't make the damn orders!"

Clarke took a deep breath, his eyes fixed on the captain's, barely holding back his frustration. He turned wildly and left.

Hayward persisted. "Perhaps ... perhaps the colonel is not aware of the full extent—"

"The colonel is not blind, man!"

There was a moment of seething silence, after which Hayward turned to go.

Hayward had expected the captain to shout something after him, but when he glanced back on his way out he saw the captain staring at his hands folded between his knees.

Clarke was waiting for him at the end of the passageway. He said nothing, nor did he react when Hayward emitted a bitter curse under his breath.

"The man never had time for me before, why should I have expected it now?"

"The Great Push is in motion. There's no slowing it down, Allan. What do we matter? We're one regiment. There's plenty more to call up behind us."

Hayward stiffened, feeling the knot in his stomach grow harder. He stared at Clarke, pushing at him to offer something more. Clarke stared back.

"I'm going to see the colonel," Hayward declared.

With effort, Clarke said, "You're daft. He'd have you committed."

"Are you coming?"

"He'll not listen to a word."

Hayward left Clarke, his warning hanging there, with some embarrassment at faltering when such brazen nerve showed in his friend.

Clarke went after him.

He caught up with Hayward, just as the fellow turned along the section of trench designated for the man leading the attack. Together they approached his dugout.

There they encountered a clump of anxious officers, Myers among them. They were in wait it seemed for orders from the colonel. Myers set an uneasy gaze on the two, at desperate odds as to what to make of them being there.

Hayward paid heed to no one except the fellow standing at the entrance to the dugout. "A word needed with the colonel."

"He cannot be—"

"It's urgent!"

"What is it? Who sent you?" the colonel yelled from inside.

Hayward and Clarke pushed past the fellow to where the colonel was seated, in full uniform, including his gloves and ash-stick. His chair, a proper and sturdy one, was to the side of a table covered with the prerequisite maps. His adjutant, standing nearby, peered at Hayward and Clarke with more authority than his rank would warrant. In the corner a gramophone stood in silence.

"What is it?" Only then did the colonel recognize Clarke from their encounter that evening. His impatience surged immediately. "What is it? Out with it!"

"We wish to pass on what we know, sir," said Hayward. "The situation does not look good ... as you are aware, I think, sir."

"Who in the blazes sent you?"

"No one. We thought you would want as much information as possible."

"I took the liberty of crawling out and taking a look, sir."

"Taking a look, Clarke! Under whose orders?"

"No one's, sir."

"For the good of the regiment ..." Hayward said.

The colonel rose to his feet. "Get back to your men!"

There was nothing for either to do but stand rigidly and acknowledge his authority with a salute and a dutiful "Yes, sir." They hesitated for a few seconds, hoping he would change his mind and hear them out, but they saw his scowl harden.

They turned to leave.

"Remember," the colonel barked, "I will not have the men doubting what we can do!"

They left the dugout. Myers eyed them.

From inside came the metallic ring of the field telephone.

"Yes." The colonel's voice was sharp and precise.

They all froze in anticipation of hearing what new orders Brigade had for them.

"Are they certain they're our flares, sir?"

The pause seemed endless.

"As soon as possible." His voice had lost its force.

Through the crackle of static came further word from Brigade.

"Occupy their front-line trench from Point 89 to just north of Point 60. I'm checking it on the map. Then work forward to Station Road. Yes, sir."

Those outside looked at each other, not wanting to believe it. The regiment had orders to go. Clarke cursed. Myers's eyes shut tightly.

"Does that mean independently of the Essex?" Another pause. "Yes. Independently, as soon as possible."

Surely they would take the time to have the artillery reposition itself?

"Has the enemy's front line been captured?" the colonel asked, with more urgency than ever in his voice.

The answer brought an end to the conversation. The telephone line fell silent. The wait for the colonel to speak held them rigid, islands for an eternal moment.

"The situation is not cleared up." His voice carried the weight of all his years as a soldier. "That's what he said."

Those outside could make no sense of such a statement. In their silence they urged the colonel to question it, to give voice to their frustration.

He uttered not a word of dissent. There was no call back to Brigade.

"Point 89. Five hundred yards due east,

then another 250 south."

"To Point 60, sir," said the adjutant.

"We'll do all we can."

At that Hayward and Clarke would stop no longer.

"God be with you," Myers said.

An order of the colonel hung in the air behind them as they went. "Get the company commanders here right away. We go over as soon as possible!"

TWENTY-FOUR

When Hayward and Clarke went their separate ways they knew the next time they could hope to see each other would be on the battlefield. They were silent in their handshake, and tried to look at each other as if nothing would change.

Hayward called, after Clarke had turned away, "We'll go for another swim."

Clarke glanced back, for the moment the familiar grin across his face. He turned the corner, and was gone.

"Sir." It was Bennett. He looked worried. "The men are very anxious, sir."

"The wait will soon be over."

"We're going, then?"

Hayward's look confirmed it. The corporal's face stiffened even more.

"The word has to come from the colonel," Hayward said.

"The men just want to get to it."

Hayward looked about at his men. They all were eyeing him.

He had a word for each of them, the encouragement that was his duty. There was not the fire that had sometimes been in his voice, though he would not have them think anything but that there was a job to be done and they were the men who could do it.

"Sir," said Smith, "she'll be over and done wit' soon."

Hayward expected more, but Smith went by, not able to stand still.

"He's on about hes wife and youngsters," Moss confided. "It's different when it's only yerself."

"You got it all figured."

"If yer number comes up, it comes up. There's not a damn thing can be done about it. No sense broodin'."

Hayward wished it was as simple for all of them. Their wait was in dense, impenetrable silence for the most part, though their minds had to be racing like his own. The few words that passed between them shrugged off the strain, foolery smack in the face of mountainous seas building ahead.

"The Hun knows better than to get saucy with a Newfoundlander."

"Gaff the buggers, I say, and fling 'em back where they come from."

Hayward gave word that the tot of rum due each man be passed out. Most took it eagerly, downing it in one gulp, savouring the burning warmth. Some others, Martin included, took their time, as if they had no stomach for it, the final rite that marked with certainty their plunge over the top.

When the order came to stand-to, Martin was on his feet and onto the firestep as quickly as the next man, his rifle at the ready, bayonet clamped to the muzzle, pointing skyward. His will to get through it was equal to his grip on the rifle. He would get through and, if he had to, go face to face with them in their trenches.

He was all but rid of the voices from home. He would be part of the Great Push and they'd not forget it. A fine time it would be when he'd

go on and on how he was right in the midst of
the charge.

By now his fear had turned to rock in his
stomach. He clenched it and riveted his attention to the lip of the trench and the leap that
would take him up and over. With three regiments ahead of them, and the hammering from
the artillery, what chance was there for anything
to be in their way? They said it was machine-
gun fire they'd heard, but no one knew for certain, and it had passed off now whatever it was.

His eyes closed and his forehead pressed
against the trench wall. He prayed God would
get him through. The prayer he repeated silently again and again, without lull, until it became
part of him, until it was all that filled his mind.

The weight of his pack dragged mercilessly
at his body. It became a penance, a sacrifice,
whatever His will might be. As more minutes
passed the effort to open his eyes had gone. He
sank away to His protection.

"Steady, Ned! On your feet, lad."

It was Hayward's voice. Martin opened his
eyes and discovered he had slumped down on
the firestep. He struggled back upright, with
Hayward's help, his rifle clenched as firmly as

ever. He said nothing. His head pressed against the trench wall again. His eyes shut.

"Six minutes, Ned."

He could feel a hand gripping his arm. When he looked it was Hayward on the firestep shoulder to shoulder with him, standing-to, pistol in his other hand.

Smith was on the firestep to his right, and Moss next to him, the trench bridge between the two. They stood eager for the whistle, their tin hats strapped tight, their jaws set. They uttered a gruff few words, making sport of what the next few minutes would bring. There was no thought now to anything but the regiment.

Martin could hear others on both sides of him, pitching droll insults at the Hun and betting on who would be the one to get Kathleen, the St. John's beauty who rumour had it wanted to marry the first of the regiment to get the Victoria Cross.

Martin straightened up more and tried to stretch the aching stiffness out of his shoulders. Hayward took some of the weight of his pack while Martin repositioned it to something less painful.

"The sledgehammer," he muttered, when he

had the full weight of it again.

"They all have their reasons."

"What good will it do us?"

"It gives you trouble out there, sling the bloody thing to hell!" The anger slashed the air.

Martin froze, unable to look into his face.

"Ned," Hayward said, a forced calmness in his voice. "You'll not do anything foolish. You'll have your go. You'll do your bit, lad. Don't be thinking about anyone but yourself. There's plenty more to fight after this one."

"Me mother'll see me back," Martin said. "She will, sir."

Hayward nodded.

"Yours too, sir."

He nodded again.

"A great day on the saltwater, what, Mossie?" Smith called out.

"Yes, and that it is so."

"Feel that sun on yer face, bud. Nuthin' like it."

Smith started to hum one of their old favourites while in the background the corporal declared them down to the last minute.

TWENTY-FIVE

The whistle shrieked through the swell of voices, a knife severing the last threads holding the regiment back. It came with the grave, imperious figure of the colonel rising out of his trench, sweeping over his head his ash-stick, signal to the men at the firesteps to follow him. After twenty yards he slipped into a side trench, as was expected of a regiment's commander, and fixed his eyes to what he had dutifully set in motion.

A and B Companies scrambled out at his call, a platoon of four sections at a time, in lines, set to advance at a walk, side by side. The platoon behind them made for the parapets, ready to rise up when the others had gone their forty paces.

Hayward and his men were over at the first

sound of the whistle. Not a man hesitated. Not one but bounded up, as steel-nerved as he'd been drilled to be. A few slipped back from the weight of their packs, but were boosted over the top by those behind.

"For the regiment, boys!"

"Kathleen, my sweet, 'tis you or a wooden leg!"

Hayward had no thoughts but of his men. Whatever they would come up against he would be at the head, and take the worst of it. His rage seared him, like a whip to his flesh, thrusting him on.

Martin caught his look. It clad the private with a fierceness of will, his footing that of a colt loose from the stake.

The morning's sun shone gloriously, catching the jagged line of a hundred bayonets angled at the sky. The young men of the Island, fresh stalwarts for the battlefield, took quick sighting of the French countryside. A glance to their right saw no sign of the Essex. Far beyond where they knew the enemy trenches must be rose smoke from the shelling barrage. They were on their own.

It was straight at it now for the regiment, an

awkward lunge of trench-cramped legs, hardening to the rhythm of stags striding over an open marsh.

Moss was first to get it.

The poor brute had barely heard the riotous clamour of machine-gun fire when the bullet smashed through his elbow. His rifle fell to the ground. He stumbled over it, pitching face first into the mud, hand clasped to his wound. His end of the trench bridge fell on top of him, though it was only a second before Smith had it off.

"Mossie!" Smith freed him from his pack and turned him over. "Damn bloody hell, Mossie!"

"Me number was at the top o' the list, Smit'." Already the hand covering the wound was red with seeping blood. "Leave me be. I'll make it back."

The explosion of machine-gun fire had come first from the right of them. Now it opened up on them from all parts of the enemy front. It was worse than anything Hayward had imagined. He had not seen Moss get hit, but ran back when he realized the two of them were gone from the line.

"Sorry, sir ... the bridge," Moss moaned.

The second wave had sprung up from the

parapets and was on its way toward them.
Already some of them had been struck down.

"Keep low, Moss!" Hayward yelled. "Crawl
back when you can."

"Save one o' them English nurses for me,"
Smith shouted at him.

Hayward grabbed Moss's end of the bridge.
Smith took up his own and they were gone.

They made it to their front trench, threw the
bridge down and crossed over it. Others had
jumped into the trench and were climbing out
the other side.

Martin had been about to do the same, but
found the spot clogged with the dead and the near
dead from the Welsh regiments.

"Blessed God," he said when Hayward and
Smith showed up.

"Come on!" Hayward roared at him.

He stumbled across the trench bridge and,
with them, made for the gap in the first line of
barbed wire. Around them men were dropping.
One ahead of him fell to the ground in a heap.
Martin stopped, but at the sight of a bullet hole
through the fellow's head he ran on. "God help
him," he muttered. He chased after the others,
who were almost to the wire.

The spectacle he met there numbed him beyond any response to Hayward's shouting. The narrow gap cut in the wire was blocked with bodies, and all around were the wounded in every state of hopelessness. Smith and some others were dragging the dead aside, trying to make room for the swarm of men desperate to get through. One of the dead Welshmen, his uniform caught on the wire, hung almost upright, his bare head thrown back, his jaw askew.

And still there was no let-up. The Hun were having their way, their guns fixed on the gaps in the wire. The men were felled like the caribou on the Island, channelled together by fences of toppled spruce.

The Hun sunk it in the corporal just as he made it through the third line of wire. One second he had freed himself from the pile-up of bodies, the next he was cut to the ground, a bullet lodged in his hip. He lay numbed. He tried to move and the pain savaged him. He heaved out the contents of his stomach.

Hayward tore the pack off him. He had to be moved if he wasn't to get it a second time or be trampled. The pain wrenched his face, him screeching at the Hun that they cared not a damn that he would never walk again. Hayward dragged him into a shell hole. He went back for his pack and threw it down so he could reach the water bottle.

"Too bad, sir," Bennett shouted. "The colonel, what will he think?"

"The stretcher-bearers will get you."

"The letter. Take it now." His hand went for his tunic pocket.

"You keep it. You'll do fine."

"Think so, sir? Good luck, sir." But Hayward was gone and had not heard him.

Bennett's head fell to the side. Only then did he see he was sharing the shell hole with the bullet-mangled corpse of a private from the Border Regiment.

Martin broke past the final line of wire and into no man's land. Only that he could see Smith lumbering on ahead of him was he able to keep up the pace.

"Smith!" he yelled.

Smith waved forward with a broad sweep of his arm and pushed on as if clearing a path for him. "This way, bud!" he yelled without looking back.

Scattered around them were others who had

made it through, now to face the brunt of the bullets sweeping the open ground. They trudged on, shoulders pressed forward, heads pulled into them, as if they were making their way home across a frozen harbour in the driving snow.

Martin glanced behind for Hayward, and his foot caught the black scar of a tree stump. He fell flat on his stomach, barely saving his rifle from the mud.

He did not move. The urge to push on was not enough to get him to his feet. Yet he had to do it. He would not shrink away with Smith thrusting ahead so madly. Neither was there time to claw at reasons not to move. He was on his knees and to his feet as if the colonel were watching his every move.

Hayward lunged up behind him, on the verge of screaming an order to get him upright, for the sun was glinting off the tin triangle on his pack. The Hun machine-gunners could never want for a more perfect target.

Hayward was beside him just as he started on again. "By God," Hayward shouted at him, but could utter nothing more.

No man's land, lacerated by weeks of artillery

fire and strewn with the bodies of the relentless young souls, gave them no pause. Plod on it was, and know it was what had to be done, for the Hun was the devil himself. Better to get it trying to cut the scourge from the earth than to let the filthy murderers have it their way.

"Not me!" Martin screamed. "Not me, sir!"

Artillery shells fell among them and bullets beat across the land like hell's flames and still there was no sound man but took his ground, his boots and puttees caked with the earth as if it were his very own.

For the first time their eyes fell on the Hun wire. It loomed in the distance, not the pulverized mass they were told it would be, but ominous, barely broken, a final heartless barrier. The ground that would get them to it sloped down, past a clump of trees, the lay of the land delivering the Hun their targets.

The trees were bereft of all but a few of their limbs. One tree stood out from the others, like a burial marker, around it the bodies of several of the regiment's men. Martin could see that one was Mayo Lind, the letter writer.

Smith yelled, "On with it, Ned!"

The lad ran after him, down the slope, only

to see a shell explode in front of Smith and cut him down.

It twisted the young fellow's heart. The instant the shell burst he knew Smith had it bad. He ran to him, but stopped and turned aside.

"Dear God," he muttered, and began to sink to the ground.

Hayward dragged him away. Nor could he bear it himself to see what the shrapnel had done.

They stumbled on as if to some refuge from the hellfire. Their only chance was for the machine-gunners to keep their sights fixed on the knots of C and D Company men behind them trying to find a way through the wire.

Hayward snatched a look to right and left. He saw a mere trickle of men. His eye caught the edge of a shell hole, one wide and deep enough for both of them. He motioned for Martin to follow him. He zigzagged his way toward it, past the heap of another dead man, fooling still the kiss of bullets.

They leapt into it. Machine-gun fire ripped the air above them as the mud of the hole gathered them in. They threw back their heads, their breathing that of desperate beasts, not daring now to move an inch.

They clutched the safety, kept shut their eyes, letting the demons rage at the distance. When they did allow the light, they found the heavens had covered them in a miraculous blue.

They cared not that they were soaked in mud. What mattered but their blood still pounding within them? Martin let himself fall away from his pack. He could not think he would ever want to rise again.

Hayward could feel no heart for it either. Yet there came the wrathful British army men, their voices rising at him, driving out secret whisperings of home, the caressing touch of Marie-Louise. At him like vehement prods of silver-tipped ash-sticks.

And still the noise of killing roared across the fields.

"Damn, cursed and damnable folly. What do you say, Hayward?"

Hayward could not think he was hearing it. He twisted his head toward the voice. There was Clarke, an arm's length from him. Hayward could not get out a word.

"Well done. By God, those drills paid off. Not a scratch on either of you."

There was even something of a smile across

his bloodied face.

"The captain got it, poor devil. Ordered me to take charge, sorry as he was to do it. I might have a chunk of steel in the leg, and a bit in the skull, but I made it this far. Still, there's more of our boys on the way. I'd say with luck someone might even make it to their wire."

"By God, Clarke. It's really you," Hayward blurted.

"I've not snuffed it yet, old chum."

They clenched hands. There was far from the strength in either of them that had been there when last they'd seen each other.

"Your leg, how bad is it?" said Martin.

"Can you crawl back?"

"Hayward, my man, you might have your chance to play the hero after all. We'll manage it together, the three of us."

From the look he gave Clarke it was clear Hayward's intent was to go at it again. He had heard men tramping past the shell hole.

"It'll prove nothing," yelled Clarke.

"The men are counting on me. Who can expect them to do what an officer wouldn't do himself?"

"What good are you smashed up? A piece

of shit—that's just what it'll be."

"Not a man wavered. Not one turned back. Straight into it, even you."

"The colonel must be proud," Clarke said. "Brigade, too. Praise to the bloody heavens! They'll be toasting us for as long as they live. God help us!" He laughed loudly.

Martin had lain silent through it all, listening to the two of them on about the war as if there were something to do except seize what life was left. His breathing came in rushes still, of the foul air made worse by the swelling heat of the sun. He wished his body to shrink into the hole, in ignorance of the putrid mud, emerging only when the predator had gone his way. He longed to hold his Shep, have him bare his teeth at anyone who dared torment them.

He closed his eyes and had it in his head what he would say in the letter home. It would not be long. He'd spare him no details. He could picture him when he opened it, the shudder in his voice when he read it aloud. His mother would be shocked and have her cry and there would be no end to the fuss about the house. Some might not think him man enough still for the regiment, but not so his father.

Then he thought of Smith. He held his Shep
harder and cursed again and again under his
breath with a fierceness to horrify the man
reading the letter.

TWENTY-SIX

Like a demonic sword it came, without warning, out of the sky. It struck to the side of Clarke. When he uncovered himself from the dirt that rained down, Hayward's heart constricted, a fist-hard knot pulled tight within his chest.

Hayward stared at the shrapnel gash in Clarke's skull, his ungodly stare, his blood oozing into his hair and draining through the dirt covering his forehead.

"Not now, chum." He reached a hand to Clarke's face and brushed closed the eyelids with his fingers. "Laugh at them again, the old fools."

He drew the hand down his face and let it rest on his friend's chest.

"Is he, sir?"

"He was the best sort. He should have been allowed a fair crack at it. The Island could have done with his kind."

How is it that it all came to this? Why was all their misery and endless training for naught?

He withdrew his pistol from its case and held it flat against his own chest. He watched it rise and fall with his breathing.

"Remember the football matches, at Bannerman Park?" Martin said. "Think you older fellows would have let us play."

Hayward turned onto his stomach. He felt the sun against the back of his neck. Slowly, he raised himself clear of the mud. He lifted his head and peered above the edge of the shell hole. For a second he was poised, gauging the intensity of the fight.

He shot to his feet and up from the hole, lunging as if submerged in water. "Now!" he yelled. "Come on, Neddy Martin, if you're to be a bloody officer!"

Hayward raced toward the Hun wire, his pistol at the end of an outstretched arm, zigzagging his way over the gnarled and blackened field. He railed at the machine-gunners in their trenches. "Godforsaken swine!" he screamed.

With another few strides he would have reached the wire.

A bullet struck the hand that held the pistol. The gun flew past his head, a spray of blood striking his face. The hit tore him off balance. He stumbled sideways. A second bullet ripped open his leg and he crumpled to the ground.

Martin, out of the shell hole and sprinting after him, saw it all. He ran without his pack, his rifle held loosely in one hand. Bullets tore the air around him, but he escaped them all. At reaching Hayward, he flung himself flat to the ground.

"It was no use," Hayward moaned. "I just wanted to see one of them."

"Your leg."

A shell struck nearby, warning them to get out of the open. Martin looked about for a hole they could make it to.

"I can help you, sir."

But the machine-guns had no mercy. Bullets swept across the two of them.

Neither man gave up. Hayward tried to push himself along the ground with his good leg, Martin dragging him as best he could. At the rim of a shell hole the private fell in and pulled

Hayward in on top of him.

He freed himself and lifted Hayward's head from the mud.

"Sir?"

He knew the moment Hayward died. It was without sound or struggle. It was his sorrowful face settling back into the mud.

TWENTY-SEVEN

Only later did Martin concern himself with his own wound. The bullet had grazed the jaw bone, below his ear. The pain grew more and more severe, and he knew he would have to bandage it. He found field dressing in Hayward's haversack.

For a time the machine-gun fire continued, but eventually it passed away. The shellfire, too, relented. Silence fell where chaos had been, the only sound the reluctant moaning of men not yet dead.

He curled away. The wait for nightfall dragged him into a stupor. But when the darkness came he drew himself out of the hole and began to crawl back toward his lines.

Again and again he passed wounded men, in states far more wretched than his own. He promised he would send the stretcher-bearers. Getting back through his own wire was the worst of it.

Near dawn he made it to the front-line trench. He fell into the arms of men from a regiment he did not know, who called him a brave young soul and told him what a fine account of themselves the Newfoundlanders had given.

They handed him a cigarette and sat him down on a firestep. He rested there for a long time, telling them of the others. He did not want to leave the spot, but after a time he got to his feet and found the way to the aid post off St. John's Road.

ACKNOWLEDGEMENTS

I gratefully acknowledge the Canada Council, for assistance during the writing of this book, and Memorial University of Newfoundland, for my term as writer-in-residence.

No Man's Land is fiction, but the battle that led me to write the book is not. I am very thankful for a number of sources that provided essential background information for the story, the most important of these being: "Beaumont Hamel" by Major A. Raley (*The Veteran Magazine,* Sept. 1921); *The Fighting Newfoundlander* by G.W.L. Nicholson; *What Became of Corporal Pittman?* by Joy Cave; *The Letters of Mayo Lind;* the diary of Owen Steele (unpublished); *Death's Men* by Denis Winter; *Songs and Slang of the British Soldier 1914–1918* by John Brophy and Eric Partridge; and *Vie et Traditions Populaires en Picardie* by Jean-Francois Leblond and Yvan Brohard.

I extend sincere thanks to the staff of the institutions where much of the research was undertaken—in St. John's: Memorial University (the Archives and the Centre for Newfoundland

Studies) and the Provincial Archives of Newfoundland and Labrador; in London: the Imperial War Museum and the Public Records Office.

I very much appreciated the assistance of Steve Austin (warden at Beaumont Hamel Memorial Park); residents of Louvencourt, France; Aidan Ryan, for access to notes made by his father, John Ryan; and Anne, John, Sandra, and Shaun, who read the manuscript and provided many insightful comments.

And to Walter Tobin, ninety-seven, the only soldier of the battle still with us, I offer thanks for his observations about the manuscript. The remarkable courage shown by him and his fellow soldiers on the morning of July 1, 1916 will always be with us.

Walter Tobin died on September 15, 1995.